But ~~he could not let her get close.~~

She had left him once, and she'd do it again.

Michael shrugged his shoulders. "I don't know what Sharla's father is thinking. He says he's gotten his act together, and now that Sharla is motherless she should live with him."

"So, he's really serious about suing for custody?" Josie asked. "What does your attorney say?"

"That my chances are fifty-fifty at best."

"If I can help... You know I would."

"I appreciate your offer. Actually there is something you could do." Taking a deep breath, Michael said a quick prayer before putting his heart in Josie's hand.

"You can marry me."

CRYSTAL STOVALL

dreamed of writing inspirational romances from the moment she discovered Grace Livingston Hill's novels as a teenager. These books changed her life in a profound way, starting her on a quest to blend faith and romance in her personal life, as well as launching her writing career. She's a graduate of Oral Roberts University and a recipient of the Romance Writers of America's Golden Heart Award.

Crystal lives in Tulsa with her husband, Jim, who is president of the Emmy Award-winning Narrative Television Network. Though she's lived in Oklahoma for nearly twenty years, she's still an Easterner at heart. Her frequent visits to her upstate New York hometown—especially a certain boulder on the edge of Cayuga Lake—provide her with the inspiration and perspective which she finds essential to her writing.

With All Josie's Heart
Crystal Stovall

Love Inspired®

Published by Steeple Hill Books™

STEEPLE HILL BOOKS

Steeple Hill™

ISBN 0-373-87133-3

WITH ALL JOSIE'S HEART

Copyright © 2001 by Crystal Stovall

Visit us at www.steeplehill.com

Printed in U.S.A.

Let love and faithfulness never leave you;
bind them around your neck, write them
on the tablet of your heart.

—*Proverbs* 3:3

In memory of my mother, Jozell Smith,
whose love lives on in my heart and
whose smile won't be forgotten.

Chapter One

This was the last place she expected to be.

Josie Marshall took a deep breath, then knocked on Michael's front door. Just past five o'clock, the late-afternoon sun cast a long shadow across the wide porch. Potted geraniums and begonias lined the wooden rail, emitting a sweet fragrance that might have calmed her nerves on another day.

For the last seven years, Josie had successfully avoided Michael Rawlins, and she'd had no intention of seeing her parents' next door neighbor on this trip home either. Yet, here she was, holding the basket of hot food her mother had prepared, waiting for Michael to open the door.

All attempts to convince her mother Josie was too tired, that she needed a long shower and a good night's sleep before she faced anyone, had fallen on unsympathetic ears. An exhausting international flight fraught with delays and cramped seating was no excuse in Sarah Marshall's mind. Sarah, relying on the persistent gaze Josie clearly remembered from childhood, had asked her daughter to *please* take Michael the food. The poor man had just been released from the hospital, and Sarah would have delivered the meal herself except she'd promised to drive Gran to her four o'clock doctor's appointment and she was already late. If Josie would do this one thing for her, her mother had sworn, she would be so grateful.

Realizing it was useless to argue, Josie had given in. However, she'd procrastinated another hour before making the short trek next door.

She rang Michael's doorbell a second time and prayed there would be no answer. Quickly, she counted to ten. If Michael didn't open the door by the time she reached twenty, she was leaving.

Eighteen, nineteen, twenty... Thank you, God, she whispered.

Taking a deep breath, she turned away from the door and hurried down the wooden steps. Halfway across the lawn she heard his voice. She would have known the deep, warm timbre anywhere.

"Josie? Josie Marshall?"

For a split second, Josie considered ignoring Michael, pretending she hadn't heard him call her name. But why should she? And what was the fuss anyway?

The thought of seeing Michael had her acting like

a silly teenager. What was the harm in spending a few minutes with an old boyfriend she hadn't seen in years? She would hand him the food, make sure he was okay, chitchat for a few minutes and then leave. She would do as much for anyone else. In fact, as director of an international children's charity, she did much more than this on a daily basis for countless strangers.

Josie took a deep breath. The truth was, not only did she need a hot bath and good night's sleep before seeing Michael, she needed a haircut, a new dress and a ten-pound weight loss. But it was too late for any of those luxuries. Making certain her brightest smile was in place, she faced him.

Michael stood on the front porch, his tall, lean body holding the screen door open. He looked the same, and yet he had changed. The longer, rebellious hair style had been replaced with a short, layered cut that emphasized his friendly brown eyes and high cheekbones. Instead of the blue jeans and T-shirt she remembered him always wearing, he looked surprisingly comfortable in casual slacks, a cotton shirt and burgundy loafers.

"Hello, Michael," she slowly answered. "If this is a bad time…" She hoped he would accept her offer to end this encounter before it started.

"Not at all. Come on in." He waved her toward the house as if he'd been expecting her.

His insistence surprised her, as did his curious gaze. She was tempted to ask what he thought. Had the last seven years been as flattering to her as they had been to him?

Uneasy with entering Michael's house, she remained in the yard. With her feet on solid ground, it would be easier to keep a safe distance between him and old memories.

"I've got your dinner." In case he hadn't noticed the picnic basket, she raised it a few inches. "In fact, there's probably enough food in here to last a family of five an entire week."

Michael shook his head. "It's a crime, isn't it? More food than I can possibly eat has been delivered this afternoon, while somewhere in the world there are families who'll go hungry tonight. I imagine with your work, the unfairness must really get to you, doesn't it?"

Josie merely nodded at Michael's casual remark. He couldn't know the half of how she felt on that particular matter, and she saw no reason for sharing those private thoughts with him now. Her feelings were strictly between her and God.

Too weary for a serious conversation, she deliberately answered with a lighthearted quip. "If you want to do battle with my mother, then go ahead. I dare you to send this picnic basket back."

Michael smiled. "No way I'm messing with Sarah Marshall. At least not until I'm fully recovered."

Only then did Josie notice the tired lines framing Michael's eyes and the stiff carriage of his upper body. While there were no visible bandages or scars, her mother had said he was badly bruised and very sore.

"Where would you like me to put this?" Josie asked, suddenly aware of his physical discomfort. She rushed up the steps, and as she neared him, he tried to take the basket. But before he could, she glided past him and through the open door.

Though it'd been a long time since she'd been in the Rawlins's home, it still possessed the same welcoming air she'd remembered from her teenage years when Michael's parents had owned the house. The floral prints and lemony walls Mrs. Rawlins had loved had been replaced with subtle earth tones and plaid fabrics. Even the carpeting had been pulled up to expose beautiful hardwood floors. The Western art, tailored furniture and Persian rugs hinted at a man she no longer knew.

Making her way to the kitchen, she deposited the picnic basket on the trestle table and started unloading it.

"I can do that," Michael insisted. He reached for the casserole dish, and for a second his hands covered hers.

Josie flinched, his touch the same combination of gentleness and strength she'd remembered. Before too many old memories slipped to the surface, she turned abruptly and broke the unsettling contact.

"I wouldn't be Sarah Marshall's daughter if I didn't finish the job properly," she announced, as if his being so close had no effect on her.

Michael jokingly raised his hands shoulder high with palms facing outward. "Hey, like I said before, I'm not messing with your mother."

Josie flashed her too bright smile. "Good. Then sit down and let me do my work." As she placed the casserole dish in the oven to warm, she described the meal. "For starters, there's your favorite, cheese-stuffed meat loaf and roasted potatoes."

When she hesitated, Michael didn't notice. A long time ago meat loaf had been his favorite. Maybe it wasn't anymore.

Oh, God, she turned a silent prayer upward. *Please, help me get out of here before I say something I'll regret.*

"I'll put the coleslaw in the fridge with the applesauce. And there's a loaf of wheat bread and—ta-da—cherry pie for dessert."

Michael shook his head. "When your mother does something, she does it right."

"Yeah," Josie said. Despite all her grumblings, she had a pretty special mom. Sarah Marshall would do just about anything for her only daughter.

Michael glanced nervously at the food then back to Josie. "I can't eat all this myself. You will stay for dinner, won't you?"

The request was simple enough, but the unreadable emotion in Michael's eyes bothered her. Despite the years and distance between them, she knew him too well not to know when he was trying too hard. If he was as uncomfortable with her presence as she was in his, then why did he ask her to stay?

"That's so nice of you to offer, but I'm exhausted and you must be, too. Maybe we could get together later in the week?" Josie said, aware that once she walked out the door tonight their paths would not cross for the rest of her six-week hiatus. She would make certain of that.

"Really, I insist," Michael said. "You know how busy you are when you're home. Your mother will be dragging you to family reunions and church dinners until you'll need a vacation to recuperate from your hiatus."

"Not this time," Josie promised. "It's going to be a quiet six weeks spent with my parents." She'd already warned her mother she wanted peace and quiet. Though she hadn't told her why it was so important.

"Please stay," Michael said. "At least for a few more minutes." The same unreadable look she'd noticed before flashed across his eyes. Could he really want her to stay? Against her better judgment, she gave in to her curiosity.

"For a little while." She'd never been able to refuse Michael in the past, and even after all this time apart, she still couldn't say no.

Josie suggested they go ahead and eat. While she filled two plates, Michael poured iced tea and set place mats on the dining room table.

"The kitchen's fine," Josie called out. She didn't

want him to go to too much trouble. She didn't want
to be treated like a date. She was an old friend, the
girl next door, and she wanted to keep it like that.

"You're right. The kitchen is more comfortable.
I'm not sure why I even kept this old dining room
set. I never use it." Still, Michael continued to set
the oak trestle table that had belonged to his grandparents. Stepping back, he inspected his handiwork,
and with a look that suggested something was missing, he opened the hutch door.

"Nonsense, it's beautiful," Josie said. "Besides,
someday, when you're an old married man, you'll
sit around that big table with your children and
grandchildren and think life couldn't get any better."

The second Josie met Michael's gaze, she wished
she could have taken back the words. Was she crazy
bringing up the subject of marriage? The sooner this
meal was over, the better.

"Always the optimist," Michael said. "I'm glad
that hasn't changed." Michael held out a chair for
her, but before seating himself, he clumsily searched
through the bottom hutch drawer.

Josie waited quietly, thinking there'd been a time
when she would have responded to his comment
with honesty. But today she was content to let him
think her optimism had remained intact.

Just as she started to ask what he was looking for,
he produced two tapered candles and wrought iron

holders she recognized as having once belonged to his mother.

In patient silence, Josie watched Michael strike the match and light the ocean-blue candles. Even though the sun hadn't set, the flames flickered in the early evening light. Instantly, she recalled how their love had burned out, but unlike a candle it wasn't something that could ever be rekindled with the strike of a match.

Josie sighed with relief. She shouldn't have avoided Michael for so many years. Because it wasn't until she'd faced him tonight that she could really be certain of her heart. She no longer loved him. In this moment, all she felt for him was the lingering fondness anyone would feel for their first love.

"Shall we pray?" Michael asked.

Reaching across the table, Josie held his hand and closed her eyes.

"Dear Father," Michael prayed. "Thank you for this food and that we could be together to enjoy it. Please, protect Sharla, who I already consider as my daughter, and let her feel how much her grandmother and I love her. And grant Josie the restful hiatus she seeks." Then a little more loudly, he added, as if it were an afterthought, "May Your will be done during these next few weeks."

"Amen," Josie said. "I always like a man who knows how to say a short prayer."

Michael grinned; and for a moment it was just like

old times. Except for the silence that followed. Josie struggled to think of something to say, otherwise it would be a long meal.

"Mom told me about your accident the day before yesterday. She said Sharla wasn't hurt." And Sarah Marshall had told her a lot of other things through the years, as well. Thanks to her mother's newsy e-mails and telephone calls, Josie knew the high points in Michael's life. She knew who he had dated, when he'd bought the house from his retired parents and when Sharla had come to live with him.

"Thank God, Sharla's fine," Michael said with much relief. "She's been staying at her grandmother's this summer, and we were lounging in the front yard when she chased a neighborhood cat into the street."

"That must have been a horrible moment." Josie had chills just thinking about the child and the speeding car.

"I can't tell you how terrified I was. I didn't think I could reach her in time." But he didn't have to explain his horror, because the fear still clung to his face. "Sharla never saw the car."

"You were lucky your injuries weren't more serious." Josie closed her eyes for an instant, knowing how close Michael had come to tragedy.

"The driver had slammed on his brakes, so by the time he hit me, he wasn't going very fast."

"But fast enough."

Michael shook his head as if his cuts and bruises

were nothing. He was obviously uncomfortable being the focus of attention.

"Thank God, it's summer and school's out. How long before you'll be back on your feet?" Even though he wouldn't have to teach until the end of the summer, he most likely had a busy agenda planned for his vacation months. Michael considered teaching a year-round job, whether he was teaching his third-grade class or Sunday school.

Michael nodded. "The doc said I should take it easy for a couple of days. My injuries are more inconvenient than anything." Michael gracefully rose from the table, as if to prove his point. Pulling his wallet from his back pocket, he showed her the photograph on top.

"Sharla's first-grade picture," he said.

Michael's eyes burned bright with love and fatherly pride. The moment stole Josie's breath.

"She's your cousin Denise's daughter?" Josie said, even though she knew the answer. When Sarah had written about Denise Rubee's tragic death, Josie hadn't been surprised to learn Michael had wanted to raise the orphaned child.

He nodded.

"She's beautiful," Josie said.

"And a spitfire, too."

Michael continued to stare at the smiling photo. With her long black hair, dark-blue eyes and lightly tanned skin, the young girl physically resembled Michael.

"I was sorry to hear about Denise's death last fall. The fact that she was so young makes it even harder to accept," Josie said. The words were inadequate, but then there were no words to heal the pain death left behind. She'd witnessed too many tragedies with her work to think a few words could possibly give real peace and comfort.

When Michael shrugged his shoulders and his eyes misted over, Josie wanted to hug him, but instead she clasped her hands under the table. Michael opened his mouth as if he wanted to say something, but then changed his mind.

Josie reached for the wallet, flipping through the photographs. There were two more of Sharla, both taken recently, as well as a family shot with his parents, sisters, nieces and nephews. At one time, she'd considered herself part of this great bunch.

"How are your parents doing?" she asked. "It's been a long time since I've seen them."

"They enjoy Florida, and they especially love being near their grandchildren." She thought she detected a wistfulness in Michael's voice. He'd always adored his older sisters.

"Have you ever thought of moving closer to them? I'm sure you could get a teaching job anywhere." And any school would be lucky to have him. No one was better with children than Michael.

He shook his head. "You know me. Tulsa's my home. I can't see myself living anywhere else."

"Of course," Josie said, avoiding his gaze. She

knew that. His refusal to leave Tulsa was one of the reasons they'd broken up.

"And your sisters?" Josie said, once again filling the awkward tension. "They're doing fine?"

"Couldn't be better. They love living in Florida."

Josie popped the last bite of potato into her mouth, then took her plate to the sink. She'd stayed too long already. There was nothing left between her and Michael except old memories, and she didn't want to stir them up too much for fear she would release the old anger and bitterness as well. She would wash the dishes and leave.

Without asking if she wanted any, Michael cut the cherry pie.

"None for me," Josie said. "I'm trying to cut back."

"Really? You look great to me."

"Thank you," she said, surprised by how good his approval made her feel. Yet a little leary, too. It was almost as if he were being too nice. She shook the feelings off quickly, but noticed he still served her pie.

Stubbornly, Josie continued to wash the dishes. As she gazed out the window, a small structure, under construction in the backyard, caught her attention.

"Is that what I think it is?" she asked.

Michael came up behind her. His breath was warm on the back of her neck as he spoke. "Yeah. It's a playhouse for Sharla."

"Oh," Josie exclaimed. Grabbing a hand towel to

wipe her hands, she left the dish suds and uneaten cherry pie behind. Michael followed her into the backyard.

The June sun hit the horizon as they crossed the thick Bermuda grass. Orange-red fingers blazed across the sky, heralding the end of the day. Evening songbirds welcomed the rise of the moon as darkness approached.

"You're really building her a playhouse," Josie said with wonderment.

At the moment, it was little more than a few studs and nails. Close by lay a pile of bricks for the winding walkway, wood shingles for the roof and fancy trim pieces to complete the gingerbread look. She closed her eyes and knew exactly how the finished playhouse would look. Or at least, she saw the playhouse she'd always wanted as a child.

As Michael watched Josie, he pressed his hand against his side to ease the pain. It was silly, but he hadn't wanted her to know how much he hurt. This wasn't the reunion he'd always envisioned. In those daydreams, he was strong and healthy and ready to prove he was doing just fine without her. And he was. He'd gotten over Josie a long time ago. The trouble was he needed her help, and from the moment she'd unexpectedly appeared on his doorstep, he'd been trying to find a way all evening to broach the subject.

Perhaps the direct approach was best.

But before he could say anything more, Josie began inspecting the trim pieces and the tiny stained-glass windows he'd located at an antique store last week. She picked up the delicate multicolored glass and let the last rays of light filter through, coating her face in muted blues and pinks.

When the breeze pushed her light brown hair off of her face, Michael silently gasped at the tender beauty of her profile. Her creamy skin and pale red lips looked so lovely, and he was reminded of what might have been. And that made him edgy. Knowing it might be wiser to walk away before he said something he'd regret, he stepped up onto the plywood platform and took the window from her hands.

"I didn't realize how much you love her until I saw this," she said. As Josie met his gaze, he would have sworn she knew how it felt to love a child as her own. But then she loved a thousand children. She had put her love for children before her love for him. And now he was going to ask her to do it again.

"Yeah, she's like my own. I remember the day Denise asked me to be Sharla's godfather. Though I took the responsibility seriously, I had no idea of the commitment I was truly making. Denise and Eddie had already broken up, and so I was Denise's birthing coach. I was there when Sharla was born. I held her in my arms when she was only minutes old. I heard her first cries and saw her first smiles."

Josie nodded. She knew this. Her mother had written about Sharla's birth in detail and how Michael had stayed with Denise those first few weeks, helping her with night feedings and diaper changes. And then he'd started keeping Sharla on weekends and making sure she had her required shots and clothes for school.

"Little by little, I became her father. I didn't even see it happening. It was the most natural thing in the world."

"I can see she makes you happy."

Michael smiled. "That doesn't even begin to describe my feelings. She's the reason I get up in the morning. She's the reason I look forward to the future."

And now it was the future that worried him.

"When Denise asked me if I would become Sharla's legal guardian, I was scared by the responsibility, but deep down I knew God had placed me in this child's life for a reason. She needed me. She needed the stability and love I could give her. I think deep down Denise somehow knew she would never beat her drug addiction. You know, she died of an overdose?" Michael's voice cracked, and he paused to regain control.

Watching Denise succumb to her illegal drug addiction had been one of the hardest things he'd ever done. He'd tried to help her, but his best efforts combined with the help of family and friends hadn't been enough. "Loving Sharla is the easiest thing I've ever done."

"I'm glad everything is working out for you."

Josie's eyes were sincere and that touched him. "Sharla couldn't be in better hands."

"It's not that simple." Michael turned away from her. He had to ask her now, before he lost his nerve. For Sharla's sake, he couldn't blow this.

"What's going on?" she asked.

"I've got to go to court later in the summer. I may not get custody of Sharla."

"What?" Josie shouted. "I can't believe this. If it was Denise's last wish for you to raise her daughter, and she had sole custody..."

Michael appreciated Josie's indignation. It made him believe she would help him.

"As it turned out, she didn't have sole custody. But because Eddie Lewis had never shown a smidgen of interest in Sharla, Denise hadn't thought it necessary to ask the court to grant her sole custody."

"And now he wants to raise her?" Josie filled in the missing pieces. "But why?"

Michael wasn't prepared to tell Josie everything. This was his fight. While he needed her help, he couldn't let her get too close in the process. She'd left him once, and she'd do it again.

He shrugged his shoulders. "I don't know what that man is thinking. He says he's gotten his act together, and now that Sharla is motherless she should live with him. He's recently remarried and has stepchildren near Sharla's age."

"So he's really serious about this?" Josie said. Michael nodded. "What does your attorney say?"

"That my chances are fifty-fifty at best. The judge hearing the case is known for siding with the biological parent."

"Wow." Josie swallowed so hard Michael saw her Adam's apple bob.

"If I can help...in any way...you know I would. Perhaps I could testify at the court hearing on your behalf?"

"I appreciate your offer to help. And actually there is something you could do." Michael said the words quickly before he lost his nerve.

"What? Tell me?" Josie gently touched his elbow, the simple gesture giving him the courage he needed.

Taking a deep breath, Michael said a quick prayer before putting his heart in Josie's hand. "You can marry me."

Chapter Two

With a thousand stars blinking in the summer sky, the only light Michael cared about smoldered in Josie's eyes.

For what seemed like an eternity, she remained frozen in place, too stunned to move. When she met his gaze, he felt the full force of her indignation. Perspiration spread across Michael's forehead and neck, and he felt as if he were melting into the black shadows cast by the outdoor lights.

"Let me make sure I heard you correctly." She took a deep breath, then pointed her index finger at him. "You just asked me to marry you."

Michael nodded his head. "I know it sounds crazy—"

"Crazy?" Josie grabbed the top of her head with both hands as she grimaced. "Crazy doesn't even begin to describe what this is. You…me…getting married? Well, it's...it's insane. That's what it is...insane." Josie clinched both fists. With each word she said, her voice became higher and louder and more agitated, while her face turned one shade of red after another.

"Okay, if you could just settle down, and let me explain—" *Dear God,* Michael prayed, *let her see my heart. I know if she would just listen she would understand and help me.* Michael reached out to take her hand, but she flinched to avoid his touch.

"Tell me this," she said, taking one more step backward. "Do you love me?"

Though he didn't speak immediately, he boldly met her gaze. "It's not that simple."

"Well, it ought to be," she whispered. Obviously unwilling to consider his request, she turned to walk away. This time when Michael reached for her, he caught her arm and brought her to a halt. If he had to beg, he would.

"If after you've heard everything, and you still want to say no, then so be it. But at least give me a chance to explain."

The seconds ticked by, seeming like hours to Michael. Doubt began to rise in his heart, followed quickly by humiliation. He'd been foolish to put his future in Josie Marshall's hands. He should have learned his lesson the first time.

Finally, Josie nodded.

He saw the reluctance, but he didn't care. She was giving him a chance, and he couldn't blow it.

"This is the only way I know to protect Sharla," he began.

It was the desperation in Michael's eyes that finally convinced Josie to listen.

"I'm fighting Sharla's newly married biological father. And I'm a single man. You know what that means. The decision could come down to those facts alone. I just can't sit by and do nothing."

"You would marry a woman you don't love for Sharla's sake?" Josie asked. Were they really having this discussion?

"Yes," he said firmly.

Josie sighed. "There has to be some other way. You've got a good attorney. You're the only father Sharla has ever known. Surely that has to count."

"It does, but I need more than maybes. I need to do everything I can to keep Sharla."

"Why?" For some reason it seemed important to know the depth of his conviction.

"Because I believe, without a doubt, I'm the best person to raise her. God brought her into my life, and I don't think He brought us together just to take her away now."

Josie glanced down at the ground, kicking the grass with her toe before looking back up. "Sharla is a lucky girl."

Still, Josie wasn't even close to being convinced she was the answer to his problems. Shaking her head ever so slightly, she feared Michael wouldn't let her say no and walk away. He was prepared to wear her down until she gave in.

"There must be another way. I'm sure there are lots of women who would jump at the chance to marry you." Michael cocked his head in disbelief, but Josie continued. "What about Marianne Blade or Julie Sparks? They're both crazy about you."

Josie saw the confused look flash across Michael's eyes. He knew there was something odd about what she'd just said, but in this intense moment he couldn't put his finger on it. But she knew. Though she'd always pretended she didn't care what Michael was doing, she'd paid attention to every bit of news her mother had passed along.

"You don't get it," Michael said. "You're the only woman I can believably marry on such short notice."

"Because we were once engaged," Josie finished his sentence.

"This marriage has to be convincing." Michael took her hands into his, as if he believed he'd already won her over. "We've got to be so real your parents, our friends, the court's caseworker, don't suspect a thing. I know we can do this, Josie." Michael paused for a minute. "Please. Help me. Help Sharla."

The word *no* perched on the tip of her tongue, and she had been ready to spit it out until he'd said: *Please, help Sharla.*

Sharla. A little girl she didn't know, but a little girl who needed her help just as Angelina once had.

For a second, she imagined Angelina's sweet, round face. Mentally she ran her fingertips across the child's smooth tanned cheeks, then through her long dark hair. She heard her innocent laughter ring out across the night sky, and she shivered.

"Please," Michael said again in a voice so low, so quiet, she barely heard him. Yet, he spoke with such intensity and determination his voice could have traveled around the world and back and she would have still heard him.

Josie once again looked her former fiancé in the eyes. There had been a time when she would have done anything for him. But this?

Again Angelina's face flashed through her memory.

She couldn't say yes, but neither could she say no.

Without giving him an answer, Josie ran.

Michael hesitated, and then chased after Josie. When he rounded the tall, thick shrubs separating the Rawlins and Marshall properties, she was nowhere to be seen. He listened for her footsteps, the slamming of the porch door, the hum of a car motor, but heard nothing. She'd vanished. Just as she had disappeared from his life seven years ago.

He'd been a fool to think she would help him.

Seven years ago, she'd put her needs and her

dreams before his, and now history was repeating itself.

Michael looked up at the nighttime sky. He'd been so certain Josie was the answer to his prayers. Had he misheard God? Or was he so blindsided by his own desires he'd interpreted God's guiding to suit his own wishes?

Sitting down on the backyard swing, Michael released a fierce sigh, suddenly feeling a sharp pain in his side. But as harrowing as this spasm was, he knew it would be nothing compared to the pain he would feel if he lost custody of Sharla.

He needed to hear Sharla's voice.

By the time he reached the back patio, the pain had subsided to a mere ache. The doctor had warned he would be stiff and sore for a few days, but that he would feel better by the end of the week, if he was careful not to overdo. He had every intention of following orders, because he needed to be in top mental and physical shape in order to convince the court he was real daddy material.

Michael glanced at the clock. It was after nine o'clock, a little later than he usually called to wish Sharla sweet dreams. Being a summer night, though, he was certain she would still be awake.

Sharla answered on the first ring. "I knew your ring," she said, then giggled before Michael could even say hello.

"You did? I think you're pulling my leg. You

looked at the caller ID box and saw my number."
The cheerful play temporarily eased Michael's mind.

"No, I didn't." Sharla giggled again. "But
Grandma did."

"You didn't fool me." He imagined her sitting
on the living room couch with bare feet and her just-
showered hair dripping on fresh cotton pajamas. He
could almost smell the baby shampoo and the
lavender soap she loved.

Every day, he missed her more. Months before
Denise's death, Sharla had moved in with him when
her mother's addiction prevented her from properly
taking care of her child. The bond between Michael
and Sharla had deepened quickly during those days
as he'd sheltered the child from her mother's ugly
habit. He wanted Sharla home yesterday.

"Daddy?" she asked. The endearment pierced his
heart, as he knew what she was going to ask before
she spoke.

"Yes, sweetheart, what is it?" His heart rate
quickened and his palms grew clammy.

"When can I come home?"

Michael squeezed the telephone cord tightly. He
would never forget the day he'd told Sharla she
would have to live with her grandmother until the
judge decided whether her permanent home would
be with him or Eddie. Even though her grandmother's home was only a half hour drive away, she
had clung to him and cried until his heart broke.

"You'll be home soon. In the meantime, I want

you to have fun with your grandmother.'' He wanted to promise her she would be home, sleeping in her sunshine-yellow bedroom at the top of the stairs by the end of summer, but he knew better than to assure her of things he had no control over.

''This summer is going to fly by. That I can promise you,'' he said.

''It's already going fast,'' Sharla said, indicating her fears had been temporarily appeased. Unfortunately, her blind faith only made Michael more anxious. Sharla was counting on him, trusting him with her heart, and he couldn't let her down.

Somehow, someway, he would gain custody of her. Even if it meant begging Josie to marry him.

Fearing Michael might follow her, Josie had slipped into the shadow of a large oak tree and had waited while he searched the dimly lit yard. Her breaths had come so loud and fast she'd been certain he would hear her. But after a few minutes, he'd turned and walked away.

He'd let her go without a fight. Just like he'd let her go seven years ago. It was good to be reminded certain things had not changed and never would.

Eager to avoid her mother's curiosity, she'd quietly entered the house and tiptoed up the stairway. Once in her bedroom, she'd undressed in the dark and slipped under the covers. Only a few minutes had passed when Sarah knocked on her door.

A thin ray of hall light branded the darkness as Sarah opened the door a crack.

"Are you all right, dear?" her mother whispered.

"I'm just exhausted. The jet lag has caught up with me and plowed me down." Josie crossed her fingers, hoping Sarah would accept the excuse without question.

"Michael said to thank you and to let you know he's going to be fine. He'll be stiff and sore for a couple of days, but he should be back to a normal schedule by the end of the week."

"You had a nice visit then?" Sarah gently probed.

"Very nice." Josie responded with enough enthusiasm to please her mother. "I'm really beat. Do you think we could talk in the morning?"

"Of course, dear. I'm just so thrilled to have you home."

"And I'm so glad to be here." Josie hated shutting her mother out. She would have loved to chat until the early morning hours as they usually did on her first night home. But Sarah would want to know all about her talk with Michael, and that was a topic she intended to avoid.

Sarah paused at the door. "Love you."

"Love you, too."

Josie waited ten minutes before turning on the bedside lamp. How could she sleep when Michael had asked her to marry him?

If her mother ever found out there'd been a second proposal...

It should have been so simple. When Michael had said he needed her to marry him, she should have said no. She didn't love him anymore, and she hadn't loved him in a long time.

But the situation wasn't that simple. And what he couldn't know is that her indecision had little to do with what they had once felt for each other and everything to do with a little girl she had failed.

Logically, she knew helping Sharla wouldn't make up for Angelina's death. However, her heart believed otherwise. Ironically, she'd come home seeking peace between herself and God, with the hope of finally putting to rest her insatiable need to help every needy child she met as a means of personal restitution.

When Josie closed her eyes, she saw Angelina's wide smile. She heard her merry laughter. She smelled her favorite peppermint candy. After six months, the images of the little girl she'd fought so hard to save were still laden with pain.

Kneeling at the side of her bed, in the exact spot where she'd prayed as a child, she talked to God. *Lord, please give me the courage to say no.*

Maybe this was some kind of test.

Feeling a measure of strength, Josie dressed, then sneaked out of the house.

As she knocked on the front door a second time that night, Josie couldn't help but reflect on how she'd once considered this white clapboard house a second home.

Michael answered the door quickly. "I just happened to look out the window and see you cross the driveway," he explained, as if he'd guessed what she was thinking. There'd been a time when they'd been so in sync that they had finished each other's sentences and had known without looking when the other had entered or left a room.

Without a word, Josie headed straight for the living room where only a small lamp burned. In the dim light, she wouldn't be able to read the emotion on Michael's face. She could tell him no and leave without feeling guilty.

This is not my problem, she reminded herself. Michael is a capable man. God will help him find another way to gain custody of Sharla.

"There's no use putting this off," Josie began.

Michael switched on a bright floor lamp, and with the harsh light, her resolve wavered. Behind the hope lurking in his eyes, she sensed a bitter anger waiting to explode.

"You need more time to think this over," Michael insisted.

"No, time isn't going to change my mind. You'll find a way to help Sharla."

"You don't understand. There isn't any other way. You are the only person who can help us. And unless you marry me, who knows what will happen?"

The anguish in his voice clawed at her heart. She could only imagine how desperate he had to be to ask her to marry him. He'd never been a man to act on impulse or whimsy. He was the most logical and dependable man she'd ever known, and he would never have suggested such a preposterous idea unless it was his last resort.

Still, she hated that he'd put her in this difficult situation. It wasn't fair. Looking away from Michael, her gaze fell upon a series of framed photographs of Michael and Sharla. They were scattered across the fireplace mantel, the coffee table and the built-in bookcases. Then she saw the Barbie backpack in the corner and nearby it was a stack of *The Baby-Sitters Club* books. Why she hadn't noticed these things immediately, she wasn't sure. But it was suddenly clear that this was Sharla's home, as much as it was Michael's.

She was still determined to say no until her gaze met Michael's.

Before she could speak, he said, "If you're willing to travel halfway around the world to save children, is it really too much to ask you to save the girl next door?"

Josie froze. He had no idea how deeply his twisted logic had pierced her heart.

"Sleep on it," he urged.

"Please, don't put this burden on me, Michael," she said.

* * *

Giving up on sleep, Josie unlocked the antique trunk that had sat at the foot of her bed since she was a teenager. The black trunk had belonged to Gran, her mother's mother, and had traveled around the world and back home many times. It was Gran who had nurtured Josie's desire to work with less fortunate children. Following in this beloved woman's footsteps had seemed like the most natural thing in the world. Though she'd had no idea then how much that decision would cost her.

The stiff hinges creaked with age as Josie lifted the lid and propped it open with a pillow. This was her treasure chest, though there were few items in it with material value. On top, wrapped securely, she found a delicate lead crystal angel Gran had sent her from Ireland, and below it, a beautiful hand-painted tea set from England. Both were things she planned to one day display in her own home.

Lately, she'd been having thoughts of settling down and getting married, starting a family of her own. But not one of those daydreams had included Michael Rawlins.

Josie slowly dug to the bottom of the trunk, respectful of the memories she disturbed. She felt the bundle of letters before she saw them, and chills traveled up her arms the minute she touched the sheaves of yellowed paper.

Slowly, as if she feared they might crumble, she pulled them to the top of the trunk, then carefully untied the pale-blue ribbon that bound the past. Sitting cross-legged on the floor, she began to randomly read the letters. The loving words took her back to another time, a time when she had loved Michael with her whole heart.

Even though she resented his forcing her into such an awkward situation, she understood he sought her help because of the depth of love they had once known. Was it possible she somehow owed it to him to say yes?

No, she didn't think she owed him anything. At least, nothing like this. But still, she couldn't walk away from his plea. What if she turned him down and he lost custody of Sharla? Could she live with that? Yet, were there any guarantees he would be granted custody even if they did marry?

With a blanket in tow, Josie moved to the spacious window seat where she snuggled amongst her childhood stuffed animals and dolls. On every trip home, she offered to pack her things and store them in the attic. Her mother always refused, somehow understanding what a comfort it was to Josie to come home to familiar surroundings.

In this room, she'd learned to pray as a child. Diligently, her mother had taught her to be thankful for the good times and to seek God in the difficult. Each night before sleep she had thanked God for her parents and good teachers and plenty of food. When she was older, and her cat had died, she'd prayed God would take care of Whiskers. Her first real challenge had been the death of her grandfather. Holding her mother's hand, she had sat by this window and prayed to God for understanding and to ease her pain. And He had heard her. She'd felt His comfort and His love. But those had been simpler times with less complicated prayers.

Tonight, as she looked toward the heavens, knocking on God's prayer door, no one answered. For a long time, she sat in silence, trying to make sense of her feelings, but coming to no real conclusion.

It wasn't right to marry a man she didn't love— no matter how honorable the reason. With that thought, Josie finally fell asleep with her head resting on a tattered teddy bear.

Late-morning sun and shrill laughter woke her. She stretched her neck from side to side, working out the kinks, then lifted her hands above her head while flexing her shoulders. Her muscles were cramped by the tight quarters, and her head felt heavy from troubled sleep.

When she heard the laughter a second time, Josie parted the sheer curtain and looked down on Michael's yard. She recognized Sharla instantly. One long, dark braid adorned with bright-purple ribbons hung down the child's back. Judging by her matching shorts, T-shirt and sandals, she adored purple.

With a huff, Sharla deposited a flat of begonias near the side of the house. Near a long flower bed that had recently been prepared for planting, bags of mulch waited to complete the job. A few seconds later, Michael appeared with another flat of flowers.

Using her hand as a sun visor, Sharla looked at Michael. "How many flowers will it take?"

"You tell me." Michael dusted his hands against the backside of his jeans.

Pressing her ear against the window in order to hear better, Josie smiled. Michael was forever the teacher.

Sharla shrugged her shoulders. "It's going to take a lot of flowers."

Turning their backs to Josie, Michael and Sharla measured off a few feet of bed and then pointed to the first flat of flowers. They measured off a second strip, and he pointed to the next flat. This continued until they reached the end of the bed. Using her fingers to count with, Sharla arrived at a number and Michael beamed with approval.

Time slipped away as the two worked. Michael dug the holes, and Sharla shoved the small plants into the soil. Together they pushed the dirt around the base of each plant, working their way toward the end of the flower bed.

When loose hair hung across Sharla's face, Michael smoothed it back into place. The second Michael pointed at a hoe or trowel, Sharla eagerly retrieved it. They didn't seem uncomfortable in the growing heat. They were a team. Even from a second-story window, the trust and understanding between the man and child were clear.

Though Josie kept thinking she needed to take a shower and see what her parents had planned for the day, she couldn't tear herself away from the window. Finally, the flowers were planted, and Michael turned the hose on to water them. It started out innocently, but within minutes the hose was flinging back and forth, and both Sharla and Michael were drenched. Their joyous screams raised goose bumps on the back of Josie's neck. The love between Michael and Sharla was so strong she could feel it. It was so compelling she longed to be a part of it.

Josie took a deep breath. She had her answer. She knew what she had to do.

The sun had set, and the sky was darkening by the time Michael returned from dropping Sharla off at her grandmother's. Josie waited for him on his back steps.

Michael slowed his pace as soon as he saw her. Though he quickly squared his shoulders and raised his chin, he was unable to hide the dejected look in his eyes. After spending the day with Sharla, he had to miss her fiercely at night.

"I didn't know you were such a gardener," she said.

"There are a lot of things you don't know about me."

While that might be true, it was obvious he was

still a good man at heart. That was one of the reasons she'd made the decision she had.

"We need to talk," she said.

Keeping a short distance between them, he said, "Go ahead."

Looking up at him made her uncomfortable, so she stood, too. She wanted them to be on level ground. "I didn't sleep much last night."

He tapped his foot with impatience, silently urging her to cut the chitchat.

"I can't marry you, Michael." When he turned away, she grabbed his arm, because it was important he hear her out.

"Marriage is sacred. We both believe that. Even if I said yes, I don't think you would go through with it. You don't love me, and I don't love you. At least, we don't love each other in the way a man and woman should love each other. And we're the type of people who believe marriage is forever. So where would that leave us when this is all over? And how could that be good for any of us—especially Sharla?"

She didn't pause long enough for him to answer because she had to finish before she lost her nerve.

"But I want to help." Michael met her gaze, and she saw the glimmer of hope. He was so desperate he would accept any scrap she would toss his way.

"I don't see what you can do—"

"I can accept your marriage proposal, and for the next six weeks we can pretend to be engaged. By that time, you should have received custody of Sharla, and I'll go back to work.''

Michael stared at her in disbelief. ''You'll do that?''

She nodded. It was crazy, but she would do it. ''For Sharla,'' she reminded him. *And for Angelina,* she thought.

When her words finally sunk in, his laughter filled the air. Michael grabbed her by the waist and pulled her close. If it hadn't been for the pain in his chest, they might have danced across the lawn. Unprepared for how good it would feel to be in his arms again, Josie closed her eyes to stop the dizziness, and prayed she'd made the right decision.

For the next six weeks she would once again be Michael's fiancée. It was a role she'd survived once. How difficult could it be to do it again?

Time became meaningless as Michael continued to hold her. His enthusiasm was contagious, and Josie found herself breathing in sync with his every breath.

Above them, the stars became pinpoints of light, while the moon climbed toward its high perch. Though the summer evening was quiet, Josie heard music. She heard a symphony of hope and peace.

When their gazes met, the song in Josie's heart faded to silence. Without thinking she leaned forward, meeting Michael halfway. She felt his breath on her mouth and down the front of her throat. She swallowed. A horn honked in the distance, and Josie came back to the present.

She pulled away, quickly covering her mouth with her hand.

"I'm so sorry," she said. "I was lost in time..."

"Yeah, me, too."

They continued to look at each other, neither daring to put words to all the feelings that had just passed between them.

"Let's just forget this happened," Michael suggested.

"That's a good idea. We were just caught up in an old memory."

Josie wanted to run, but that would be like saying she was afraid of Michael. And she wasn't. But she was afraid of the way she had once loved him. The old memories weren't buried as deeply in her heart as she'd thought, and tonight had proved that.

She let her gaze circle the backyard, and it all came back to her. Michael had proposed to her the first time, right here on this very spot. It, too, had been a summer night filled with moonlight and promise.

"If you think you can't handle this," Michael said, "tell me now, and you can walk away."

Josie didn't look at him immediately. The wise thing to do would be to bow out gracefully, but that would be the same as admitting she was still enamored with him. And she wasn't. She just hadn't expected to be blasted with so many feelings from the past. The raw emotion had caught her off guard, that's all.

Josie took a deep breath and thinking of both Sharla and Angelina she said, "I promised to help you, and I will."

Chapter Three

She'd made a huge mistake.

Josie pulled the covers over her head and disappeared into darkness. It was a bad dream. A very bad dream. That's all. She would drift back to sleep, and when she woke up, she would be plain, old, unengaged Josie Marshall again.

A few minutes later, she cautiously peeked out from beneath the covers, but nothing had changed.

"Ooh," Josie grumbled as she punched the pillow. "I can do this," she told herself. "If I keep things simple, it won't be that difficult," she mumbled. She would play the role of Michael's fiancée when needed, and then the rest of the time she would focus on the real reason she'd needed this unscheduled hiatus.

With her bedroom door partly open, the delicious smells of bacon and biscuits drifted up the stairway.

Her mouth watered, prompting her to get dressed and join her parents for breakfast.

At the top of the stairs, she paused. Her parents' voices were low enough that she couldn't follow their conversation clearly, but the bits and pieces that traveled through the otherwise quiet house were light and teasing, tender and loving. Only eighteen months ago, she'd flown home from London to help them celebrate their thirtieth wedding anniversary.

No one had ever had to tell her the love her parents shared was special, a rare commodity these days. They had the kind of relationship she dreamed of having one day. A long time ago, she'd believed she'd found that kind of love with Michael, but they had been too young, too immature to hold on to it.

It wouldn't be easy for her and Michael to fool her parents. If only there were another way she could help Michael and Sharla.

Josie started down the stairway, then on impulse rushed back to her room and dialed Michael's number.

"Good morning," Michael said. At the sound of his warm, cheery voice Josie sighed with relief when she didn't feel a tug in her heart. Until that moment, she hadn't realized how desperately she needed proof that the emotions his embrace had evoked last night were merely remnants from their past.

"Hello," Michael repeated.

"It's Josie," she said. "We've got to talk."

"I'll be right over," he said, then quickly hung up the telephone.

"No, Michael. Wait," she quietly yelled.

Even though she heard dial tone, she kept on talking. "I don't want you to come over here. I don't want us to spend any more time together than necessary. But we have to have a plan or this phony engagement is going to backfire on all of us."

She glared at the telephone and then punched her pillow.

By the time she entered the kitchen, Michael had already joined her parents at the table. Her mother served him a large plate of scrambled eggs just the way he loved them—smothered in hot salsa.

"Good morning, pumpkin." Her father hugged her and kissed her on the cheek. "I've got an early meeting this morning, so I'm off. But I'll see you at dinner tonight."

"I can't wait." Josie smiled, thinking how pleasant it would be to spend a quiet evening with her parents.

John Marshall winked, and then he was gone.

Sarah poured Michael a cup of strong coffee, then followed her husband to the front door.

In a loud whisper, Josie said, "You've got to get out of here."

"And pass up my favorite breakfast? No way." Michael added cream to his coffee.

"We need to talk before this goes any further," Josie insisted. With her frustration level rising, and her parents saying their goodbyes nearby, she feared she would say something she might later regret.

"We do need to talk," he said, meeting her gaze.

She relaxed a little.

"But after breakfast."

"Michael!" Where did he find the nerve to barge into her home? She'd agreed to be his pretend fiancée; she hadn't agreed to hand over control of her life.

Josie silently drummed her fingers on the table while Michael cleaned his plate and ate a second biscuit. When he'd finished his meal and her mother still hadn't returned to the kitchen, Josie realized Sarah Marshall was up to her old tricks. Sarah had always believed Josie and Michael belonged together. It seemed the old dream might still be alive.

When Sarah did return, Michael spoke up. "Josie and I were just thinking of taking a walk at River Park. Would you like to join us?"

"I would love to, but I've promised to take Gran to the grocery store." Then turning to Josie, she added, "She'll be joining us for dinner tonight."

"I was hoping she would feel up to a night out. I'm planning to stop by and see her this afternoon." It was hard to believe *her* Gran now resided in an assisted living home.

"She's anxious to see you, too, dear, but I think it would be best to let her rest this afternoon."

"Okay." There would be plenty of time to visit with Gran later. And she intended to have many long talks with the beloved woman. No one ever understood her like Gran did.

Even before her mother spoke, Josie knew by the sparkle in Sarah's eye she wasn't going to be pleased.

"Michael, if you don't have plans for this evening, why don't you join us?"

Michael looked to Josie who stood just behind her mother. She shook her head slowly, making sure he understood she didn't want him at her homecoming dinner.

With his gaze set on Josie, he said, "Mrs. Marshall, I'd love to come to dinner."

If he'd been within reach, Josie would have put her hands on his shoulders and shaken him.

They didn't speak again until they were in the car and halfway to the park, which followed the Arkansas River through Tulsa.

"If I were you, Michael," she said, "I wouldn't forget that I'm doing you a favor."

"Is that a threat?" With one hand casually draped over the steering wheel, Michael looked cool. But Josie knew better. She noticed the twitch of his chin and the nervous way he pushed his fingers through his hair. He wasn't half as confident as he acted.

"No. It's just a reminder." She softened a bit as she thought of Sharla and all that was at stake for Michael.

"Think about it," he urged. "Remember how things used to be between us?"

Though she nodded her head, she resisted thoughts of the past. In the last two days, she'd already been bombarded by more forgotten moments than she cared to relive.

"Remember how I used to barge in on Saturday mornings and your mom would invite me to eat breakfast with her and your father while you were still upstairs sleeping?" As Josie nodded, a vivid image of a younger Michael popped into her mind. "Remember how we used to argue about the silliest things, but neither one of us ever stayed mad?" Again Josie nodded.

"And your point?" she said, eager to end this forced stroll down memory lane.

"Your parents and our friends are going to expect us to act the way we used to, and when we do, they'll believe we're still in love."

"You have it all figured out," she muttered.

Michael sighed. "No, Josie. I haven't even begun to figure anything out."

Josie bit down on her lip. She wanted to tell Michael everything would work out, but she new better. The court might not grant Michael custody of Sharla. He might fail the child, just as Josie had failed Angelina. And as she had for the last six months, Michael would question his faith. Did God really listen to our prayers? Were His answers always for the best? When a child had died in your arms, it was hard to trust in God's wisdom again.

Michael turned off Riverside Drive and parked

near the fountain and pedestrian bridge at Thirty-First Street. Here, the Arkansas River cut a half-mile-wide ribbon through the west edge of Tulsa. Alive with turtles and dragon flies, the full river flowed south between banks edged with willowy trees and spring flowers. In the distance, a lonely, long-legged gray egret perched on weathered driftwood.

Michael led the way onto the bridge, which had once belonged to the railroad. The dark, wooden trestle structure with its plank floor loomed massive and sturdy. The farther they walked over the river, the stronger the June wind blew. Below them, water roared over the low-water dam, making it difficult to talk.

As they neared the small pavilion that marked the halfway point on the bridge, Josie increased the pace. She wanted to pass by the landmark to prove the old memories had lost their value, but Michael had other ideas.

"Do you mind?" he asked, pointing to a bench.

She was about to urge him to keep walking when she noticed the way his hand pressed against his back. "This would be fine," she agreed.

For a moment, they stood at the railing, looking north toward the Twenty-First Street bridge and the downtown Tulsa skyline. When Josie had first left home, this was the image she'd carried in her mind. Without doubt, it was one of the most tranquil places in Tulsa. Especially now, with the June flowers in bloom. But after she'd realized she and Michael would never get back together, it was an image she had purged from her heart. Here on this very spot, where they stood right now, Michael had kissed her for the first time.

Josie refused to look at him until her memories were under control. If they were going to spend time together this summer, she would have to get used to this topsy-turvy feeling, because it wouldn't matter where they went, there would be old memories waiting for them.

"I think we need to get a few things settled," she began, purposely avoiding his gaze by looking down at the swift river.

"I've been thinking, too."

When she did face him, the worry in his eyes concerned her. His thoughts were of Sharla, not long-ago kisses.

"With Sharla spending the summer at her grandmother's, I'm hoping we can get through the next six weeks without telling her about our engagement." Michael leaned against the railing for support.

"I believe that's wise. This pretend engagement would only confuse Sharla." And if it'd already turned Josie's heart upside down, what effect would it have on a six-year-old?

"I don't see any point in telling my parents or sisters, either," Michael added.

"The fewer people who have to know, the better,'' Josie agreed. ''We're doing this for Sharla, not to hurt her. I won't forget that.'' These next six weeks weren't about their past, they were about a little girl's future.

Michael squeezed Josie's shoulder. ''You'll never know how much your support means to me.''

''Oh, I think I do.''

Something about the tone of Josie's voice caught Michael's attention. The solemn look in her blue eyes convinced him she understood exactly how he felt. He wondered what had happened to her that would give her such compassion. Then he warned himself that it was none of his business. He could appreciate Josie's kindness without getting involved in her life.

''We'll have to tell your parents, of course,'' he said.

''Convincing them we're in love isn't going to be easy. They've written the book on a good marriage,'' Josie said.

''Plus I'll have to find a way to keep my mother from calling yours to discuss wedding plans. But that really shouldn't be a problem. Since your parents moved to Florida, our families only keep in touch at Christmas.''

''They're not going to be too happy with us when they find out this is all an act.'' He'd realized that at the breakfast table. In less than five minutes, the Marshall family had once again welcomed him into the family fold.

"If you don't mind, I don't think we should ever tell them, or anyone else for that fact, that this is all a hoax." Josie's wide eyes convincingly pleaded her case.

"But we do have to break up," he said firmly. He wanted to be clear on that. He wasn't interested in turning back the clock. She'd left him once before, and he knew given a second chance, she would leave him again. God had given her dreams that didn't include him.

"Of course we have to break up," she said. The indignation in her voice comforted him. "I'm perfectly clear on our deal. I can't believe you thought—"

"Just clearing the air," he interrupted before the situation spun out of hand.

"What I started to say was that we should just break up in a very public way. We should be able to convince everyone we'd simply been overcome with old memories, and we really weren't in love after all."

Michael couldn't have said it better himself. All morning old images had been popping into his mind. And as he looked at Josie now, he couldn't help but remember the nervous boy who'd kissed her for the first time in this very spot. His palms became clammy just thinking about that awkward moment from long ago. But like she'd said, that was their past. There was nothing between them now. He couldn't even call them friends. All he knew about her life were the exciting tidbits Sarah Marshall relayed. But there was more to Josie's life than her mother guessed. The sadness he glimpsed from time to time in her blue eyes betrayed secrets no one knew.

"Yeah, we should have a fight in front of your parents, so there won't be any doubts in their mind," he said.

Josie nodded.

"But in the meantime, we have to convince them we're falling in love. And to do that, I think we have to spend some time together. I don't think we can just walk into dinner tonight and tell them we're getting married."

"So what do you suggest?" Josie's nose and mouth crinkled with misgivings.

"They need to know we're together. Every day. Just like this. Nothing formal. Just casual dates," Michael said with confidence.

"A few hours a day would be enough, don't you think?" Josie hugged her arms to her chest, as if the thought of spending time with him repulsed her.

"I think so." Michael continued as if he had her full support and confidence.

"And what matters is that they think we're together."

Michael nodded, wondering the direction her mind had taken.

"Let's say we came here tomorrow or even met at a restaurant. We could spend the time reading or working, so it wouldn't be as much of an inconvenience to either of us. I know you're on vacation, but I'm sure you'll have to take some time this summer to write next year's school plans.''

The idea appealed to him. ''That's fine with me.''

Josie smiled for the first time that morning, and her beauty amazed him. Her loveliness went far beyond pretty eyes and silky hair. Only a woman with heart would have agreed to his harebrained scheme. Once again, he felt the old frustration and anger rise within him. They should have been married. They should have had children by now. Instead, they were both alone. Though he would always be grateful for her help, he would never forget the little faith she'd had in their love.

Checking his watch, he said, ''It's time to go home.''

As eager to leave the bridge as he was, Josie matched his pace. The morning had convinced Michael of one thing. This would be the longest six weeks of his life.

After the morning on the bridge, Michael regretted inviting himself to dinner. His mischievous mood at breakfast had backfired on himself. He'd been ribbing Josie, trying to get a rise out of her, and all because he'd wanted to keep her off balance. However, the little time they'd spent on the bridge earlier proved that in order to survive this engagement they had to stay at arm's length.

"Michael, please sit here. And Josie next to him. Let's see, Gran, why don't you come around here?"

Sarah Marshall was too busy orchestrating the seating to notice the reluctant steps of her daughter and Michael. When Gran popped up between them, both Josie and Michael smiled.

Sarah frowned.

"If you don't mind, I would like to sit between my two favorite people and let their youth rub off on me." Gran grinned as she reached for both Josie's and Michael's hands. "Who's going to say the blessing?"

"Would you, Gran?" Josie encouraged.

"Dear Lord," the older woman began. "Thank You for this food and this precious time together. May the blessing of love unite us tonight. Amen."

Though she was used to Gran's short, direct prayers, Josie also knew a cryptic message often lurked behind her well-chosen words. *Let love unite us tonight.* Josie let her gaze drift around the wide table. Yes, she thought, attaching her own spin to the prayer as she avoided her grandmother's probing eyes. In the days to come, let love reunite me in a very special way with my family.

Demanding everyone's attention, her father launched into a funny story he'd heard at work, and for a short time Josie forgot her secret engagement.

After dinner, they moved into the living room, where Sarah served coffee and Josie's favorite date cookies. Only when Gran announced her old bones needed to go home, did Josie realize how quickly the evening had passed. Being surrounded by the people she loved comforted her, and she hated for the evening to end. She'd even enjoyed Michael's presence.

"If you'd let me, Gran, I'd be happy to drive you home," Michael said.

"I haven't had a better offer in twenty years." Gran winked.

As soon as the two had left, Josie felt her parents' gaze before she even looked at them.

"It's good to see you and Michael together again." Her father pulled her mother close to his side.

"I enjoyed the evening, too," she said, hoping to satisfy her father's curiosity.

"He looks well," her mother added. "You'd never know he'd been in an accident."

"God was watching out for him. He's still a little stiff, but in another few days, he should be back to normal." Josie hated to cut the evening short, but she would if her parents insisted on talking about Michael.

"Your mother said you spent the morning with Michael."

Josie hoped to sound casual. "He needed to stretch his legs, so we went for a walk. It was good to catch up."

"You know he's always welcome here," her father said, though the approval in his eyes suggested much more.

Josie gathered her nerve and seized the moment. "I hope you mean that. You may be seeing a lot of Michael this summer."

As shock and pleasure crossed her parents' faces, Josie tried to tell herself she was doing the right thing for the right reason.

When Josie went down for breakfast the next morning, she noticed an extra plate of eggs and salsa.

"I thought Michael might stop by," her mother explained.

"I'm sorry," Josie said. "I should have told you our plans aren't until later today. We're having lunch together."

Sarah smiled and all was forgiven.

As soon as breakfast was over, Josie rushed upstairs to call Michael.

"Couldn't wait to see me, huh?" he teased.

"Can you be serious for once?"

"Maybe you're the one who needs to lighten up."

"Nobody is listening to us, Michael. We don't have to have one of those silly arguments you described yesterday."

"Okay. I'll take you to lunch."

"No, that's not what I said. We'll go Dutch, and I want to drive."

"You'll borrow your mother's car?"

"No, I want to drive yours."

"In your dreams," he said.

"Don't you wish," she teased back. If they could maintain this lighthearted sparring they might have a chance of getting through their charade.

At noon, Michael backed his Jeep Cherokee out of the garage and honked the horn. Josie raced out of the house and directly to the driver's side. When Michael showed no signs of moving, she tapped on the glass until Michael lowered the window.

"You're serious about driving?" A weary look darkened his eyes. She nodded. "Been there and done that."

"I can't believe you're still holding a grudge. It's been ten years since the fender bender." That accident had been her fault, but if she hadn't been so enthralled with the good-looking boy seated next to her, she would have seen the parked truck.

"It was more than a fender bender. My car was never the same." And Michael had never let her drive his car again.

"Fine. Then you can forget lunch." She crossed her arms over her chest and refused to move.

"All right," he finally agreed.

She hopped in, waited until they had both buckled up, and then shifted the car into Reverse. She hit the gas pedal hard and the car zoomed to the end of the driveway. She stomped on the brakes, and they lurched to a stop.

"Whiplash," Michael called out.

Josie grinned.

Michael rolled his eyes. "Tell me again why I'm going to let you drive my brand-new Jeep?"

"Show a little trust, Michael. This is what any good fiancé would do."

"Of course...that goes without saying."

By the time they reached the main street, Josie had adjusted to the feel of the new car and drove with ease.

She glanced over at Michael. "Thanks for letting me take the wheel."

"I'd forgotten you probably don't get to drive much. Do you even own a car?"

"No. My apartment in London is a short train ride from the home offices. And when I'm visiting foreign sites, I hire a car or rely on a local contact to provide a driver. It's funny the things I get homesick for. Like driving on the right side of the road in the country. Or strolling around Swan Lake. Or shopping at Woodland Hills Mall."

"What else do you miss?"

Because he seemed genuinely interested, she continued her wish list. "Most of all, I miss long talks with Mom and Gran. I miss eating dinner with my parents. I miss knowing everyone who lives on the block. And I miss sitting in a church on Sunday morning where I'm surrounded by people I've grown up with." Feeling suddenly vulnerable, Josie pretended to concentrate on the traffic ahead.

Good thing she'd stopped herself, or she would

have told him she'd been missing Tulsa so much she was thinking about coming home, and if she found the right person, settling down and starting a family.

"We'll do those things," he said.

"Oh, Michael. I wasn't trying to—"

"I know," he interrupted. "But we need to spend time together. Why not kill two birds with one stone?"

"I'd just as soon not kill any birds."

She glanced at Michael, and when he smiled she did, too.

Without warning, huge raindrops splashed the windshield.

"Seems like a good day for the mall," he said.

"But don't you want to eat first?"

"I'm betting you were too embarrassed to admit you still love fast food."

Josie blushed.

"We'll eat at the food court."

Josie turned south, toward Woodland Hills Mall. Having spent hours hanging out there as a teenager, she could have driven to the intersection of Seventy-First Street and Memorial with her eyes closed. The recent mall renovations immediately impressed her. The cool marble floors, palm trees and skylights gave a spacious feeling. Most of all, she loved the white carousel located in the center of the mall.

A half hour later, Josie felt full and satisfied and suggested they work off the cinnamon roll she'd devoured for dessert.

Walking at a slow pace, they hadn't gone far when they ran into several church members and then three of Michael's previous students. Everyone welcomed Josie home and asked if she was here to stay. Each time, she coyishly hemmed and hawed, and people smiled knowingly. Speculation that Josie and Michael were back together would be the hot rumor by the end of the night.

They had walked in silence for a short distance when Michael asked, "Why did you come home this month?"

"To see my parents." He gazed at her with wise eyes she tried to ignore. "I missed my parents, and the charity I work for is going through some reorganization. So, it seemed like a good time to come home."

Michael nodded his head, but she knew he still believed there was more. She hadn't planned on confiding in him, but she did want to talk to someone, and he seemed willing to listen.

"I'm thinking about making a change, and I wanted to take some time to reflect and pray and seek God's direction for my life." She wouldn't tell him why she needed to make a change. That was between her and God.

"I hope you find the answers you seek," he said.

When she realized he wasn't going to encourage her to explain or offer any advice, she felt hurt. But it was for the best, she told herself. They had no business getting involved in each other's lives. Things were already too tangled as they were.

They continued to walk toward the carousel, the familiar music growing louder.

"I dare you to ride," she said.

"I'll take the challenge," Michael said with the grin she loved.

They each bought a ticket and mounted side-by-side horses. The crisp organ music began again, and Josie laughed with sheer joy as the horses moved up and down.

Life was like that, she thought. Sometimes you went up and down and around in circles, but if you kept praying and seeking God, eventually you found your answer.

She didn't know what the future held for her, but as she looked into Michael's eyes, she saw the past and all the mistakes she'd made. Goose bumps marked her arms as she suddenly knew this was part of the reason God had led her home. She needed to look back at the past and examine her mistakes.

She smiled at Michael, certain he was one mistake she wouldn't repeat.

Chapter Four

"Jooo-siiie. Josie Marshall. Come in, Josie Marshall." Michael snapped his fingers in front of Josie's nose. "Where'd you go?"

Josie slapped her thighs, then said, "I'm sorry. I don't know if I can do this."

Michael's face grew rigid with anger, then he turned and walked away, as if he were afraid of exploding. Josie swallowed hard. It had seemed like a good idea to spend the next afternoon at Michael's, practicing how they were going to tell Josie's parents *the good news*. But the more approaches they'd tried, the more nervous Josie had become.

She dreaded telling her parents she'd accepted Michael's proposal. Had she known her parents still harbored hope of her and Michael rekindling their former romance, she would never have agreed to help Michael and Sharla—at least in this way. However she looked at it, she was deceiving the two people who loved her most. Only last night, she'd made Michael vow once again to *never* ever tell anyone their engagement was purely for show.

Michael marched back into the room and shoved a framed photograph into Josie's hand. Letting her index finger trace the innocent profile, she studied Sharla's beautiful smile. "This isn't fair," she said.

"What's not fair is having this child uprooted and torn from the only life she's ever known. I've loved Sharla from the moment she was born. I'm her father, and I'll do what it takes to keep her."

Josie exhaled, then set the photo on the table. "Okay, let's try this again."

From time to time, she glanced at the photograph. The child's laughing eyes and wide smile demanded her attention. In time, she realized the trust she saw in Sharla's countenance reminded her of the trust she'd once seen in Angelina's eyes.

Out of habit, the old prayer found its way to her lips. *Dear Lord, please let me help this child in the way I couldn't help Angelina. Let me make up for my past mistakes through Sharla.*

Josie lost all concentration of the task at hand. She'd come home intending to make peace with God, yet with the best of intentions, she had wound up back in the same old rut. How was she ever going to find her way back to the faith and trust she'd once known?

Michael sighed. "Josie, you've got to concentrate."

"I'm sorry. What were you saying?"

"I think we should tell them tomorrow night. We can't put this off any longer."

Josie leaned back in the chair and closed her eyes. This was her last chance to back out. Once they told her parents, she was locked in to the role of fiancée.

What should she do? She hated second guessing herself. She was tired of rehashing the pros and cons. It all boiled down to one question: Did she want to help Sharla? And the answer was simple. Yes.

"You're right. We'll tell them tomorrow. And let's tell them at home. I don't want to risk a big scene at a restaurant." Josie could see it now: her mother standing on a chair shouting, "Josie and Michael are getting married!" All of Tulsa would know before the morning paper was delivered.

"I could invite everyone here," Michael suggested.

"Since when did you learn to cook?" Josie instantly recalled the one meal Michael had prepared for her. At the time, she'd been so in love she hadn't cared that the mashed potatoes were lumpy, or that the chicken casserole had been charred beyond recognition.

"I've learned a few new tricks," he insisted. "But you do have a point."

"Mom will be thrilled to cook."

"I second the motion."

"And let's wait until dessert to drop the bomb."

"No argument here," Michael quickly agreed. "If we tell them too soon, we'll have to discuss wedding plans all night."

"That has to be avoided at all costs." Josie leaned back in the chair grateful she and Michael were in sync on this matter. As long as they both remembered why they were doing this, everything would fall into place. It had to.

"You know," Josie said, feeling bolder, "it would never have worked between us."

"Yeah, we were lucky to find that out before we became a divorce statistic." Michael relaxed, stretching his arms over his head. The worry lines that had etched his face all afternoon disappeared.

"Can you even imagine us together?" Josie laughed as if this were the most outrageous idea she'd ever heard.

"Never would have worked." Michael laughed, too. "For starters, you're a vegetarian, and there is nothing I love more than a big, juicy steak."

"Ooh," Josie said. "Well, you would have had to cook your own meat, that's for sure. Or with my great persuasive skills, I would have converted you within the first month."

"Fat chance."

"With the way you cook, it wouldn't have taken that long."

"You might be right on that."

"And really there are some great vegetarian recipes—"

"I'm not giving up meat," he said.

"Right. Well, look at our tastes. They still haven't changed much." His questioning gaze prompted her to explain. "I can tell by the way you've decorated this house. Very predictable, Michael. You're very predictable."

"So now you're criticizing my house?" He looked around as if he truly thought something might be dreadfully wrong with the decor choices he'd made.

"Not at all. It's just not what I would have chosen."

"Then it's a good thing you don't live here," he reminded her. "But what's not to like?"

"It's not a question of likes and dislikes. This is a very traditional house, and you've brought in very contemporary furniture and colors. It works, it's just not what I would have selected."

"How would you have decorated this house?" He leaned forward, as if she were going to impart great words of wisdom.

"What I would do is beside the point. You like contemporary architecture. I love old castles. The two don't mix."

Michael looked at her thoughtfully, then said. "I live in the future. You're drawn to the past."

Josie inhaled, determined to conceal her displeasure with his remark. And the fact that it upset her forced her to examine her heart. Was she stuck in the past? Was that the reason she was having so much trouble moving on and determining the direction of her life? Michael seemed to know exactly what he wanted, and she envied him that confidence.

Uneasy with the observation, she focused on another area. "You're the type who plans a trip down to the last detail."

Michael rolled his eyes. "And you're the most annoying type. You want to hop in a car and take off without reservations or even a destination in mind." Michael grimaced as he spoke.

The slight wrinkle of his nose combined with the sudden lift of his shoulders amused Josie. "It's so much more fun to follow your heart and live on the edge. To have total freedom to do what you want to do when you want to do it." Her enthusiasm grew as she spoke. "Whenever I have free time, I go exploring. I've seen the most wonderful sites, Michael."

As she told him about her excursions abroad, Michael fell under her spell. Her passionate voice drew him to faraway places where he imagined her standing in the middle of a field of heather, or saw her standing on a cliff in the north of England. In his mind, he watched her stroll through a German castle, then along the banks of the Ganges in India. She had seen a world he would never know—a world of excessive splendor as well as a world of extreme poverty—and the distance between them was so great he had no worry of them ever becoming close again.

And yet, the longer he listened to her adventures, the closer she drew him to her heart. Without realizing it, he'd moved from the chair to the sofa, until mere inches separated them. With his arm draped across the back of the sofa he could touch her shoulder, if he'd desired. And he noticed she'd angled her body toward him. While her sometimes humorous, sometimes dramatic stories entertained him, the passion in her voice and the sparkle in her eyes told the most incredible story. At heart, she was a strong, independent woman who wasn't afraid to fight for the underprivileged children she loved.

He recalled the old adage—to know your fiancée's mother is to know the woman you'll love for the rest of your life. Josie Marshall came from a long line of strong, godly women.

On its own, the old bitterness rose up within him, and Michael felt the enchanted moment slip away. Josie was wrong. Their differences had been superficial, but faith and trust had been the core of their problem. And as he looked into her eyes, he wasn't fooled by her laughter or compelling stories. Josie Marshall was as lost and confused as the day she had left him.

She's no longer my worry, he said to himself while he smiled at her story. Just because she'd agreed to help him didn't mean he was obligated to fix her life. Unless she asked. And he was confident she was too proud to ever tell him what caused the sadness in her eyes and the catch in her voice when she studied the photos of Sharla.

Josie looked at her watch and gasped. "Look at the time. I've got to go," she said. "I promised Gran I'd stop by to see her this afternoon, and I've got to tell Mom about dinner."

"I'll see you tomorrow at six," he said. Sharla had asked to go to the zoo, and he'd promised to spend the whole day with her. He couldn't wait.

"We'll tell Mom and Daddy after dessert," Josie confirmed. Though she tried to sound confident, her voice wavered.

Michael nodded. "It'll be a breeze. You'll see," he insisted.

After he closed the door, Michael leaned against the wall and prayed they would make it through the evening. So much depended on their convincing performance.

"Let's have a barbecue," Sarah Marshall exclaimed. Then misinterpreting her daughter's disapproving look, she added, "I can grill a few garden burgers along with the steaks. But this is short notice, and there's so much to plan. I think we should wait for the weekend. I've got to decide on the guest list and the menu, not to mention the shopping, cleaning and actual cooking." Sarah retrieved a pad and pen from the cabinet drawer and began jotting down notes.

Josie gently stilled her mother's pen. "I'm talking about something simple. Just family."

"I know, dear," Sarah said. "But I was talking with Jean Wilson this morning, and she mentioned that she would love to see you. And Genell Crane cornered me the day before at the grocery store. So we can invite them, and the Kramers, too. That way, everyone will be happy." Sarah began writing again.

And most of all, Sarah Marshall would be happy.

"I'll make a deal with you," Josie said. Behind her back, she crossed her fingers and prayed this bargain wouldn't come back to haunt her. "We'll have a party later. But tomorrow night, I want to be with family. You, Dad, Gran, and if you wouldn't mind, Michael."

Her mother looked up, setting the pen aside. "Of course. A nice quiet family dinner," Sarah said. "That would be lovely."

Josie would have had to be blind not to see the pleasure spread from her mother's eyes to her lips. In an attempt to hedge off the myriad of questions her mother was certain to ask, Josie said, "I'll be happy to do the shopping tomorrow morning."

"That would be a huge help. I've promised to take Gran to the ladies' prayer group tomorrow morning, and I would hate for her to miss it. But I'll still do the cooking."

Sarah hugged her daughter and then began pulling down tattered cookbooks and making more notes. If Josie hadn't known better, she would have thought by her mother's enthusiasm that Sarah was planning a wedding.

Josie gulped. The pretend engagement would be a breeze compared to the breakup. Thankfully, when the day came, she would be halfway around the world from Sarah's disappointment.

By six o'clock the next evening, Josie had changed her outfit for the barbecue for the third time. Nothing seemed to look right. Jeans were too casual. The diaphanous dress suggested she cared more than she did. The slacks didn't feel good. With clothes scattered across the bed, she finally grabbed a short navy skirt and white T-shirt with a summer sweater that she tied over her shoulders. She slipped into a pair of flat sandals, then scrutinized her choice in the mirror. When she made the A-okay sign, her reflection gave her the thumbs-up.

Even though she was running late, Josie took a second to inhale deeply and pray. *Dear God,* she whispered, *please help us get through this evening. Please let me remember what it was like to be in love with Michael so I can pretend to love him again.*

From out of nowhere, Gran's sage voice barged into her mind. "Be careful what you wish for, child. You just might get it."

Josie's heart rate quickened, and she opened her eyes. She was all alone. She'd heard Gran's warning so many times, she'd merely imagined her presence.

One more glance in the mirror, a quick adjustment to her sweater, and Josie headed downstairs. Laughter and happy chatter drifted through the glass patio doors. Her parents, Gran and Michael were crowded around the grill. When her father patted Michael on the shoulder, Gran winked at both men. To any stranger, they would have looked like a happy family.

"There you are," Michael called out as soon as she stepped outside. Without hesitation, he kissed her on the cheek. She looked at him and smiled, and then felt a painful tremor travel to the deepest regions of her heart, as she suddenly remembered how wonderful it had been to love this man.

As she studied his profile, she realized he possessed all the traits she still looked for in a man. He was loyal and kind and compassionate. He was funny and warmhearted. And above all, he had an unwavering faith she envied.

Yet with everything going for them, they still hadn't been able to make it work. Their dreams had taken them in different directions. Still, she wondered what he would think if he knew she questioned those dreams and the choices they'd led her to make. What would he think if he knew she might not go back to London? Josie bit her lip, stopping the ridiculous thoughts. She was going back to London in six weeks. She loved her work. It was her life.

"Is anyone else chilly or is it just me?" Sarah asked.

"I'm a little cool," Gran said.

The balmy afternoon air had grown colder by the hour. Thunderstorms, which had been forecast for later in the evening, were moving in more quickly than anticipated.

"Let's move this barbecue indoors," Mr. Marshall suggested.

"Josie, Michael, clear the picnic table," Sarah Marshall ordered. "John, please take care of the grill. I'll help Mother in."

Working as a team, the Marshall family quickly moved indoors, taking the joyous mood to the dining room table. Holding hands, Mr. Marshall thanked God for good food, the rain and for this precious time with his daughter.

Gran struck her spoon against the water glass. "Hear, hear," she said. "We're not letting you get back on that plane without the promise you'll come home more often. Telephone calls and e-mails are great, but they're nothing like having you here with us."

Josie looked from Gran to her parents and her heart overflowed with love. In the last few years, it had become increasingly harder to leave. While she loved her work, a huge part of her regretted the time she missed with her family. In the last few days, she'd become more aware of Gran's advancing age and the toll it exacted from her mother. She felt guilty leaving this entire burden to Sarah. She should be here to help. Yet, until she heard clearly from

God, she wouldn't make any changes. Just because the separation was difficult, didn't mean God hadn't called her to work with children around the world.

"I'll put it in writing, Gran," Josie said. "I'll do my best to get home more often. I miss you all so much."

Sarah took a sip of water and then set her glass on the table. "There are children in Tulsa who need your help," she said quietly.

"True." This was not a new argument. Sarah worried constantly about her daughter's health and safety abroad. As a faithful prayer warrior, she stood guard against everything from terrorist attacks to third-world diseases.

Michael leaned forward, resting his arm across the back of Josie's chair. "I think this is a good time to tell them the news."

Josie's eyes widened. How could he do this to her? This wasn't the way they'd rehearsed the plan. They were supposed to wait until after Sarah had served the chocolate brownies.

"What news?" Sarah asked. Josie stole a glance at her parents, unable to meet their curious, yet hopeful stares.

"I think I've got a way to keep Josie closer to home," Michael said.

Josie kicked him hard on the shin. His brows drew together, convincing her he didn't have a clue that the harm he was about to inflict upon her parents could never be undone. Now, Josie was going to break her family's heart twice. First when she told them she wasn't going to marry Michael, and then again when she boarded the plane bound for London.

"Don't keep us in suspense," Sarah said.

The room fell silent as everyone looked to Josie. She had no choice but to tell them. With her gaze settled on Michael, she took her time, forcing herself to remember the thrill she'd once felt as his fiancée.

"Michael has asked me to marry him," Josie announced. With all the nerve she could muster, she looked him directly in the eyes and smiled as if she were a woman hopelessly in love. A tiny tear pricked the corners of her eyes.

Michael put his arm around her shoulder and pulled her close. Surprisingly, the warmth of his embrace made her feel protected in this vulnerable moment.

Gran jumped up first to hug Josie. Her mother cried so hard she couldn't stand, while her father stood and extended his hand across the table. "Welcome to our family, Michael," he said as they shook hands.

"I just can't believe this is happening," Sarah said as she finally rushed around the table to hug her daughter. "I've always believed you were meant to be together. You don't know how hard I've prayed you would find your way back to each other."

"Don't stop praying for us now," Josie exclaimed, and everyone laughed. "We need your prayers now more than ever." She looked to Michael for confirmation, and he nodded. No doubt he was feeling equally overwhelmed by their emotion.

Panicked, Josie mentally searched for something to defuse the situation. Then it occurred to her. "There's something we need to clarify. I'm afraid you've gotten the wrong idea."

Michael's arm tightened around her waist as if to remind her they were doing this for Sharla.

"You're not having second thoughts already?" Sarah blurted out.

"No," Josie answered honestly. She was long past second thoughts and on to tenth and twentieth doubts. "Michael and I are engaged, but there are a lot of details to work out. We haven't decided what the future holds."

"Oh," they all said in unison, with Michael's voice the loudest.

"You've assumed we'll stay here and that may not be the case. Our charity is in great need of teachers like Michael. We would make quite a team. We've got a lot to consider." She met Michael's gaze as she spoke. He'd thought he had the upper hand when he sprung the news on her parents before dessert. Well, this should prove to him she wouldn't be manipulated.

"Yes," Gran said wisely. "You have much to think about." The knowing tone of her voice disturbed Josie. It was as if Gran knew the truth, but that was impossible. Still, Gran had always had a way of looking into Josie's soul and understanding her granddaughter.

"Well, either way, we have a wedding to plan," Sarah said brightly.

"Let's just celebrate the engagement tonight, dear," John said.

Josie was quick to agree. "We'll have plenty of time to plan the wedding. Let's savor this moment."

"We need a photograph," Gran said.

"Why didn't I think of that?" Sarah called out as she hurried to find the camera and tripod.

"But what about dinner?" Michael asked. "It's getting cold. I hate to see all your work go to waste."

"Nonsense," Gran said. "We can eat anytime, but we can only celebrate our Josie's engagement once."

Josie looked at Michael. He knew they were in trouble. In one instant, the whole plan had slipped from their control.

Once Sarah returned with the camera and tripod, her father gathered them around Gran, set the timer on the camera, and then jumped to his wife's side. "Smile," he called out. A few seconds later, the camera flashed, and the family moment was frozen in time.

Before they moved, John said, "I would like to pray."

With all heads bowed and hands joined, Josie's

father began to pray. Opening her eyes, Josie met Michael's bewildered gaze.

"Dear Lord, we thank You for Josie and Michael and that You've seen fit to bring them back together. May their love grow stronger with each day and each challenge they face. And may they never take their love for granted, but may they grow old together with their children. Bless this union, now and forever more. Amen."

Josie cried the tears of a happy fiancée, while in her guilty heart she felt more lost and confused than ever.

The rain continued as Josie and Michael stood beneath the awning on her parents' back patio. A dim wall light pierced the stormy darkness.

"This is not going to work," Josie insisted.

"It has to," Michael said. "We can't go back now. We've told them."

"I can break up with you at any time. And they will believe it, because we've done it before."

"You set that up nicely," he said. "Where would you ever get the idea that I might join you abroad?"

Josie shook her hands in frustration. "You're so blindsided by all this. Can't you see what you've done to my family by raising their hopes that I've come home to stay? They want that more than anything."

The sudden regret in his eyes told her he understood what he'd done. "You have to believe me, I didn't do that on purpose. I love your family as if they were my own."

"That's another thing you'll have to think about when this is over. When we break up this time, my family might break up with you as well," Josie said.

"Aren't you overreacting?" Michael asked.

"I don't think so. You heard my father's prayer. He's asked God to bless this union. This isn't a game any longer. Innocent people are going to get hurt. I—I just don't know if I can do this."

Michael grabbed her by the shoulders and gently shook her. "You have to," he said. "You have to for Sharla's sake. And you have to for yourself."

"What do you mean?" she asked.

"I see it in your eyes. There's a reason you said yes that has nothing to do with me and Sharla. I would bet a million dollars it has everything to do with this unexpected hiatus."

"You're crazy," she said. He was right, but she wouldn't give him the satisfaction of telling him so. "I'll do this one thing for you, Michael. But when it's over, it's over. And I will never want to see you again."

"Fine," Michael said.

Though Josie longed to slam the porch door, she entered the house quietly so as not to disturb her parents.

Alone in her bedroom, she crawled into the window seat and stared at Michael's house. He left a trail of lights as he snapped off the porch light and made his way through the downstairs to his upstairs bedroom. Through sheer curtains, she watched his silhouette pace the room.

Thoughts of Angelina and Sharla filled her mind as she snuggled with an old quilt in the window seat. I'm doing this for the right reasons, she reminded herself. In a few more weeks, she could say goodbye to Michael and never look back again.

Eyes closed in silent prayer, Josie pressed her face against the window. She didn't want to be angry with Michael. In fact, the thought of never seeing him again scared her. They might never be close friends, but he had played too big a part in her life to cut him out completely.

When she opened her eyes, she looked directly at Michael's window where he, too, stood with his face pressed against the glass. On cue, time rolled back to their high school years. To signal a truce after they'd had a fight, each would stand at their bedroom window and blow a kiss.

Not sure if Michael would be able to see her in the dim light, Josie opened the window and then blew him a kiss. Within seconds, Michael leaned out his open window and returned the kiss.

Somehow, they would find their way through the coming weeks. They had to.

Chapter Five

"**G**o ahead. Open it," Sarah urged, pointing to a large box wrapped with wedding paper that had been placed on the white table. Pleasure as sweet as icing dripped from her smile.

"You didn't have to buy me anything," Josie said as she took her place on the back porch glider beside her mother.

"I know, but this is a special time in your life, and I want to share every minute of it with you."

Josie nodded with understanding. Due to Grandfather Marshall's poor health, her mother had been denied the wedding of her dreams. Because her parents had been married at a small family wedding, Sarah had always anticipated Josie's special day with great plans.

Covering her mother's hand with her own, Josie said, "Being with you is the best gift."

Tears dampened Sarah's eyes. "I miss you so much. I know I shouldn't get my hopes up...but if you could come home to live..."

"We'll see," Josie said. "This is something I...we...need to pray about." And Josie had done plenty of praying. The trouble was, she wasn't hearing any response. God seemed to have taken a hiatus, too.

She'd come home to reconnect with God, to renew her faith and to seek His direction for her life. Yet, it seemed all she'd found were more questions. In the busy confusion of the last few days, Michael had dominated her thoughts. It occurred to her that like Angelina perhaps Michael was yet another excuse she'd wedged between herself and God.

Didn't she already know what she had to do?

She needed to forgive herself.

But it wasn't that simple.

A child had died in her arms, and with Angelina's death her own world had been shaken. For the first time in her life, she questioned her faith and her work with the children's charity.

How was she ever going to sort out her life? And where did she start? How did she find her way back to God and the simple faith she'd once believed in?

"Mom, how can you be sure when you've heard from God? I mean how do you separate what you desire from what God directs?"

A gentle smile crossed Sarah's lips as she brushed a strand of brown hair from Josie's face. "Such a grown-up dilemma. Sometimes it's hard for me to believe you're no longer my little girl.''

"Trust me, it's just as hard for me to believe, too.''

Sarah took a sip of tea, giving careful consideration to her daughter's question. "There's no easy answer. When you know, you know. I think the mistake too many people make is that they look to outward situations and indicators to base their decisions on. The important decisions are made in the heart. Like your engagement to Michael. Outwardly, it doesn't appear to be the easy choice. He's built a life here, and you've built one halfway around the world. But if you know in your heart it's right to be together, then the details can be worked out.''

Josie nodded. The advice was simple: follow your heart. However, after Angelina's death, her heart had shut down, gone on strike and she couldn't seem to prod it into even the briefest conversation.

"I hope I've been of help,'' Sarah said, as she finished a piece of shortbread she'd made that morning.

"As always.'' Her mother had given her plenty to think about. Maybe she was putting too much pressure on herself by forcing God to reveal his plans for her future within her hiatus. Maybe God's timetable differed from her own. Maybe she simply needed to relax and enjoy herself and give her heart a chance to mend.

For the first time in months, Josie felt that silent

click in her soul that told her she'd made a wise decision.

She picked up the box and tore the wrapping paper off as if it were Christmas. From mounds of tissue paper, she pulled a spiral-bound hardcover book. At first she thought it was a journal or scrapbook. When she turned it over and saw her name embossed on the front cover she mustered the biggest smile she could with hopes of pleasing her mother.

"This is the most beautiful wedding planner I've ever seen," Josie said.

"I'd hoped you would like it," Sarah said. "I know it's your wedding, but we'll have such fun planning it together."

"It'll be a time we'll always remember," Josie added.

"I have so many ideas." In a burst of enthusiasm, Sarah hopped up and paced across the room. Her eyes shimmered with images of lacy wedding veils, satiny dresses with long trains, and cascading white rose bouquets.

"And I have a few ideas of my own." When Josie met her mother's gaze, she knew there would be no easy way to temper Sarah's excitement. This was a day Sarah had dreamed of, and Josie didn't have the heart to take this dream away from her. What would be the harm in planning a wedding? Hopefully, someday she'd marry. Why not plan it now?

"I've already made some notes."

When Sarah pulled several sheets of notebook paper from her skirt pocket, Josie suddenly felt trapped. Hugging the wedding planner to her chest, she frantically searched her mind for an excuse to leave, a believable reason to postpone this initial planning session.

"I think we should start with a date," Sarah continued.

"Mom," Josie interrupted. "If you don't mind, I would like to show Michael the planner before we make any decisions. I don't want him to feel left out of the process. You know how men can be." Josie rolled her eyes.

"Of course. They tell you they want to be involved, then they leave all the hard decisions and work up to you."

Josie and her mother shared a conspiratorial smile, then Josie headed to Michael's house.

Since her mother was watching, she had no choice but to knock on Michael's door. When he didn't answer, she thanked her lucky stars. Standing on tiptoe, she felt along the top of the door frame for the spare key Michael's parents had once concealed. Then using the key she found, she entered the house. No longer in her mother's sight, she returned the key, closed the solid oak door and sighed with relief.

"Michael?" she called out. "Michael, are you home?" She waited, listening for the smallest noise, and when she heard nothing she walked into the entryway. After three steps, she froze in place. She shouldn't have entered Michael's home uninvited. Trespassing was a crime. Even though she believed Michael would understand the necessity of escaping her mother's enthusiasm, she felt uncomfortable in his home.

Yet, as her gaze slowly surveyed the formal living room to her left and the dining room on her right, as well as the open stairway straight ahead, she couldn't ignore the tug from her adolescence. There had been a time when she'd come and gone from this house as if it were her own. Michael's parents had insisted on treating her as if she were family.

Lured by familiarity, Josie went into the living room. Thick rays of sunlight streamed through large windows illuminating the polished hardwood floor, leather chairs, and a series of bronzed Western sculptures. At first glance with its earthy tones, the room appeared totally masculine, but upon closer inspection Josie sensed Sharla's influence in the softer details: the three porcelain cats that stretched across the coffee table, the blooming African violets which filled the north windowsill, and the child-sized rocking chair with its needlepoint seat. Youthful energy and vitality infused the decor in the same way Sharla added life and color to Michael's world.

"Michael?" Josie called out one more time to be certain he wasn't home. Led by curiosity, she ambled through the downstairs rooms. Even though she'd told Michael she wasn't keen on his taste, she did appreciate the way he'd blended newer pieces of furniture with family heirlooms, such as the dining room set. But what truly pulled the old and the new together were the multitude of family photographs scattered throughout the rooms. Everywhere she turned she saw the smiling faces of his nieces and nephews, his sisters, his parents and of Sharla and her mother.

A dozen photos or more covered the top of the open rolltop desk that had once belonged to Michael's father. Mesmerized by the collage of the past, Josie studied each framed memory.

The instant she saw it, Josie sucked in her breath and dropped the wedding planner to the chair seat as if it were weightless. She retrieved the small frame hidden in the back. For some reason, she hadn't noticed this one the last time she'd been in the house. She recalled clearly the day this photo had been taken. She had gone with Michael's family to the lake during the summer of their freshman year at college. Perched on top of a huge boulder with their arms wrapped tightly around each other, love radiated from their eyes with the brilliancy of sunlight.

Carefully, she set the past back in its place.

But not before old memories had been dislodged.

Before she could corral her wayward thoughts, they raced to a dangerous plateau. What if she and Michael had gotten married? What would their lives be like today?

Josie let her gaze drift from the living room to the

dining room across the entryway, then down the hallway to the bright, spacious kitchen. The present blurred as what-could-have-been overtook her senses.

What if this was her home and she worked with a children's agency in Tulsa? Most certainly, she would leave work before her children—two girls— came home from school. She would race into the house, drop her briefcase in the entryway and hurry to the kitchen to fix them a quick snack. She would spread peanut butter and thick strawberry preserves on graham crackers or melt cheddar cheese on bagels—just as her mother had. On special days, they would bake cookies together and the yummy aroma would greet Michael at the back door. With no more than two steps into the house, he would call out, "Honey, I'm home." Along with the girls, she would race to his side where they would blend together in one group hug.

Then after dinner and homework, they would tuck the girls into bed and settle alone on the Persian rug in front of the fireplace. With their arms wrapped around each other, they would feel safe from the hassles of the world. Michael would look into her eyes and tell her he loved her, that he couldn't live without her. Then he would lean forward, his lips seeking hers....

The doorbell would ring.

The doorbell rang a second time, and alarmed by the urgent buzz, Josie jumped. Still enveloped by the fog of what-could-have-been, she rushed to the door and opened it, forgetting she shouldn't have been in Michael's house in the first place.

The tall woman had lovely eyes, thick long hair, and a look of confidence that Josie respected. However, as the stranger stepped into Michael's house as if she'd been there before, she stirred a pang of jealousy in Josie's heart. Though Josie had read about Michael's girlfriends in her mother's letters and e-mails, she'd never thought she would have to face the beautiful women.

"I'm here to see Michael," the woman said. "He's expecting me."

"He's not home at the moment. If you'd like to leave a message, I'll make sure he gets it." Josie began to wonder if she'd let a pushy saleswoman into the house. After living abroad, she was out of practice when it came to the fine art of avoiding door-to-door solicitors.

"I'm sorry. Where are my manners?" the woman asked. The slight blush on her cheeks confirmed her embarrassment. "It has been one long day, and it isn't over yet. But that doesn't excuse me from barging into your home."

Too busy thinking how she, herself, had barged into Michael's home, Josie missed her chance to correct the misassumption.

Extending her hand, the woman said, "I'm Anne Devon."

Josie instantly recognized the woman's name. As

the social worker assigned to Sharla's custody case, Anne would assist the court in deciding whether the girl would live with her biological father who had deserted her before birth, or with the man—who driven by love—had raised her as his own.

"And you're…" Anne prodded.

"Josie. Josie Marshall," she said quickly. "I'm Michael's fiancée." The words rolled off her tongue as if she'd practiced this role a thousand times.

"Congratulations," Anne said, seemingly pleased at the news.

But the woman's smile didn't fool Josie. She'd seen the flicker of doubt before the happy facade dropped into place. She couldn't blame her. Anne's job required her to probe beneath the surface and determine the truth. Which meant Josie and Michael would have to work all the harder to convince this officer of the court they loved each other.

Out of the corner of her eye, Josie glimpsed the wedding planner. "In fact, I'm looking for Michael myself." As she spoke, she motioned for Anne to follow her into the living room. "My mother just gave me this beautiful wedding planner, and I couldn't wait to show Michael," she gushed.

"It's beautiful." Anne gently turned the book over in her hands. She rubbed her fingers over Josie's embossed name.

"My mother is so excited. We're barely engaged, but she's already got the wedding planned," Josie babbled on.

At the sound of footsteps, they both looked up to see Michael.

"I was hoping you would be waiting for me," he said to Josie, as he kissed her on the cheek. Then turning to Anne, "It's good to see you. I assume you've met my fiancée."

"Yes, we've just met. She was showing me your beautiful wedding planner."

Josie wondered if anything ever ruffled Anne Devon's cool exterior. "A gift from Mom." Josie handed him the book, feeling as if she were putting her life into his hands.

Michael pretended to admire the planner. With his arm firmly around Josie's waist, he looked down at her and said, "All we need to do now is to set the date."

Playing the dutiful wife-to-be, Josie smiled and blushed. "I'm thinking an early fall wedding would be nice. September is such a beautiful time of the year."

"That sounds perfect. If we can wait that long." He gave her a playful squeeze, and she giggled. "We can set the date this evening. I'm sure Ms. Devon has more important matters to discuss."

Seeing an opportunity to escape Anne's watchful eye, Josie said, "I'd better get back to the house before Mother comes looking for me." Then realizing Anne might not know her parents were Michael's neighbors, she pointed to the house next door. "Michael and I grew up together."

"Please stay," Anne insisted. "As Michael's wife, you would become Sharla's stepmother should he gain custody. Your presence during my interviews is important."

"If it will help," Josie said, though she preferred leaving this discussion in Michael's capable hands.

Once Michael and Anne were seated in the living room, Josie offered to serve iced tea.

"That would be lovely, dear," Michael said.

"Nothing for me," Anne said. Glancing at her watch, she added, "This won't take long. I just had a few follow-up questions regarding our first interview."

"I want to do everything I can to speed this process along," he said, giving Anne his full attention. Then shifting his gaze, he said to Josie, "I am parched. Would you mind making me that glass of iced tea?"

"Okay," she said with hesitation, in an attempt to conceal her eagerness to leave the room.

While Anne pulled a manila folder from her briefcase, Michael anxiously watched Josie until she disappeared into the room. One wrong answer from Josie, and their plan would crash.

"Before we go over previous questions, let's start with your engagement. Surely, you know this affects the situation."

Though the caseworker's voice remained neutral, Michael didn't back down from the challenge in her eyes.

"I'm sure this all seems sudden to you." In the kitchen, the bang of cupboard doors stopped. Though he couldn't see his fiancée, Michael knew she stood just out of sight but where she could hear every word spoken between him and Anne Devon.

"Until today, I've never heard of Josie Marshall." Anne hastily scribbled a few notes on a blank sheet of paper and then stuffed it into the file folder.

Michael walked over to his grandfather's rolltop desk and retrieved the photo of himself and Josie, then handed it to Anne. "Josie and I grew up together. As kids, we were inseparable. A few years ago, we were engaged, and when our professions pulled us apart we didn't think our love was strong enough to survive the geographical distance, so we broke up." As he spoke, he continued to pull photo albums from the desk drawers. One at a time, he handed proof of the love he'd once felt for Josie to the caseworker.

"But our love did survive, and when Josie came home on hiatus last week, we knew without a doubt that we were meant to be together."

As Anne flipped through the pages of his memories, Michael felt Josie's presence. Just out of Anne's view, she stared at the photo albums. Amazement pushed her eyes wide-open. Michael averted his gaze, unwilling for Josie to witness his vulnerability. He'd never wanted her to know he had kept these albums. When she'd first left him, he'd studied them daily, looking for clues as to why their love hadn't been enough to keep them together. Then with time, they'd become a reminder of the mistake he never wanted to repeat.

He glanced at Josie, and he knew by the flinch of her body that she felt the anger burning in his eyes. They had been so right for each other, yet she'd walked away without turning back. He thought he'd forgiven her for abandoning him, but in this moment he knew he still harbored resentment.

Faking a cough, Michael cleared his throat and regained control of his emotions. Josie slipped from view, and he turned his attention back to Anne and her list of questions.

Anne stood to leave just as Josie returned with Michael's iced tea. "I'm sorry I took so long," she said, without offering a further excuse.

Anne smiled, extending her hand to Josie. "I'm pleased we had a chance to meet. We'll talk soon when I'm not so rushed."

"Anytime," Josie said, pressing next to Michael's side. "You can leave a message through Michael or reach me at my parents'."

"It will probably be next week before I call. With the custody hearing approaching, the interviews and assessments need to be completed soon."

Josie and Michael followed Anne to the door, then stood on the front porch as she walked to her car. Conscious of the caseworker's attention, Michael casually slung his arm over Josie's shoulders and pulled her closer.

Despite all the pain this woman had caused him in the past, he couldn't help but revel in the warmth of her body. He hadn't expected her to still be a perfect fit. He hadn't expected it to feel so right.

Michael kissed the top of Josie's head one more time for show, and then pushed her away before his body deceived him. Their love was in the past, he reminded himself. She'd left him before, and she would leave him again. There was no way he would ever give her a chance to break his heart again.

"By the way, how did you get into the house?" Michael asked.

"The key over the door." Josie swallowed hard enough to tip her head.

"Yeah, the key over the door." He'd forgotten all about the spare key.

"It wasn't my intention to intrude—"

"Don't worry about it," he insisted. "It all worked out for the best. Having Anne Devon catch us together can only add credibility to our story."

Michael reached up and removed the door key from its hiding place. He'd given Josie the key to his heart once before. He wouldn't give it to her again.

Chapter Six

Josie read his message loud and clear: she wasn't welcome in his home. Translated: He didn't want to spend any more time with her than absolutely necessary.

Well, neither did she.

It had been silly to think they could be friends. Too much love and disillusionment had passed between them.

"If you don't need me for anything else, I'll go home," she said.

Instantly, Michael's eyes softened. "I'm sorry. I didn't mean to be rude. I was worried Anne Devon would question our engagement."

"I understand," Josie said, as she walked away, secretly grateful for the splash of reality. She'd been so caught up in the what-could-have-been fantasy when Anne Devon had arrived that she'd actually started to believe she and Michael might still have a future together. But even before Michael had pushed her away, she'd felt his stiffness as the emotional distance between them escalated.

Michael had made it clear he wanted nothing more from her than a pretend engagement, and it was best she not get caught in the web of old feelings. Since he hadn't loved her enough the first time they were engaged to support her dreams, to follow her when she'd left, there was no reason to believe he would support her given a second chance. And she would be crazy to trust him with her heart again.

Josie wished she could confide in her mother, her grandmother or even a close friend. But she couldn't talk honestly with anyone in her family and her best girlfriend lived in London, and that telephone call would be too long and costly. Pretending to be Michael's fiancée was more complicated than she'd believed it would be.

Though she was still attracted to him, deep down she accepted that they could never rekindle the love they'd once cherished. That had been a love built on youthful dreams and idealism. Since then, they'd both grown up and moved on in opposite directions. The work they both believed God had called them to do had torn the fabric of their love that they'd once thought indestructible. Yet, no matter how many years or miles separated them, Michael would always be her first love.

As soon as Josie reached the shrubs which divided

the Rawlins' and Marshalls' properties, she turned back toward Michael's house. Surprisingly, he still stood on the porch. Though he fussed with the flower planters, she suspected he'd been watching her leave.

"They get more direct sunlight than you would expect," he called out, pointing to the wide planters filled with white and red begonia blossoms. "If I don't water them every other day, they wilt."

Turning his back toward her, he pinched dead blossoms off the lush stalks and fiddled with the dirt as Josie reapproached. Knowing her presence rattled him gave her a small amount of pleasure.

"They're almost as pretty as the geraniums your mother used to grow in these planters," she teased.

"Be nice." Michael swung around, his composure once again in place. "There's nothing wrong with these begonias."

"I never implied there was."

"As if you have a green thumb to brag about." Michael pointed at her and smiled.

"Okay, okay," she said, knowing his thoughts had returned to the summer when she'd planted a garden in her parents' backyard. She'd gotten off to such a good start. Within days the tiny vegetable and herb plants had pushed through the soil. But a slight mishap with the fertilizer had scorched the seedlings and ended her gardening dreams. "But if I remember correctly, you were the one who measured the fertilizer."

"Don't even try to blame that on me. I stirred the exact amount of granular mixture into the water that you asked for."

Josie started to laugh, and Michael did, too.

"We did some pretty crazy things back then," she said.

"Yeah," he said, the joy fading from his eyes. "But that was a long time ago. Times have changed, and so have we."

Josie nodded, though she didn't totally agree. In her heart the past felt as close as yesterday. But he was right. They'd both grown and matured in the last seven years, and there was a part of her that wondered about the man he'd become.

Through her mother's e-mails and letters she knew the essentials of his life. She knew he still attended the same church they had as children, only now he taught a children's Sunday school class as well as third grade at the elementary school they'd attended. Late at night, he loved to play the piano, while unbeknownst to him, Sarah Marshall often sneaked into his yard on clear summer nights to enjoy her favorite hymns. He dated often, but never seriously. And on Wednesday nights, he almost always ordered pizza in.

While Josie never encouraged her mother to report on Michael's comings and goings, she'd found herself looking forward to the news. But the facts her mother relayed didn't tell the whole story. They didn't reveal his dreams and goals and aspirations.

And now that their lives had crossed again for this brief stretch of time, she was more curious than ever as to the heart of this man who could not only love a child who wasn't his, but fight for her as well.

She sensed Michael's faith had deepened and grown in ways she'd yet to experience. Maybe that was another reason why God had brought them together at this time. Perhaps, if she would let her guard down just a little, Michael could help her regain the simple trust she'd once had in God.

The more she thought about it, the more convinced she became that she should get to know this new Michael. She wasn't naive enough to think his faith would just rub off on her, but she did believe if she would let go of her pride she might learn something from this man. But to do that she needed to spend quality time with him, and earlier on the porch he'd made it clear he wanted as little to do with her as necessary.

Despite her better judgment, she gave in to her curiosity and asked to see a glimpse of his everyday world. "I'd like to meet Sharla," she said.

Without hesitation, Michael looked her right in the eye and said, "No."

Three days later, Josie waited by the back door. When Michael backed out of his garage, she rushed across the lawn to greet him. As soon as he stopped the car, she opened the passenger door and hopped in.

"What are you up to?" he asked. Though he spoke abruptly, she sensed he was glad to see her.

"I told you I wanted to meet Sharla." Josie had no intentions of backing down. The more she'd thought of it, the more she'd realized the request wasn't unreasonable. And certainly, not as unreasonable as a fake engagement.

"What makes you think I'm going to see Sharla now?"

Josie checked her watch, then rolled her eyes upward. "Get real, Michael. You're as predictable as a clock. You've left to see Sharla every morning this week at this exact time. To the second."

Instead of denying her claim, he banged both palms against the top of the padded steering wheel. With his focus straight ahead, he said, "We've been through this."

"Meeting me won't hurt Sharla," she said, disputing his ongoing argument. "Besides, she already knows my parents. It's only natural she would meet me while I'm home on hiatus. You can simply introduce me as Mrs. Marshall's daughter and your old friend from high school."

Michael tilted his head as doubt dashed across his wide-open eyes. "Josie, there is nothing simple about this."

That was true. But she didn't want to discuss it with him, because to do so would mean she would have to admit this past week and a half in his presence had released old memories and feelings she'd believed were forever dormant.

"I'm not giving up, Michael. So why don't we get this over with?" She started to lose her patience.

"Why are you so determined to meet Sharla?" he demanded.

Too embarrassed to tell him the real reason, that she thought spending time with him might somehow help her regain her trust in God, she said, "I think I should meet the girl I'm helping."

Michael sighed, put the car in Reverse and backed down the driveway. "You win."

Funny, she didn't feel like either of them were winning.

"How long does it take to get to Sharla's grandmother's house?"

"About half an hour. Grandma Rubee lives on the south side of Tulsa."

"At least she's close."

"Yeah. If her grandmother had lived out of state, I don't know what I would have done. This way I can see her every day."

"And what about her biological father?" Josie knew those chance times when Michael's and Eddie's visiting schedules had collided at Mrs. Rubee's must have proved excruciating for Michael.

Frustration creased Michael's forehead. "At first he visited once a week. When he realized I spent time with Sharla every morning, he started stopping by every afternoon."

Josie cleared her throat, knowing Michael might not like what she was about to say. "It seems to me that Sharla wins no matter what the court decides."

Michael pursed his lips, taking his time to answer. "I hadn't thought of it that way."

"If Eddie is really serious about forging a real relationship with her, then even when you are awarded custody, he will continue seeing her."

A slow smile spread across Michael's lips. "Thanks for your confidence."

"What?" Josie asked, uncertain of what she'd said to garner his sudden praise, but pleased nonetheless.

"You said *when* I was awarded custody, not *if.*"

"You're the best father for Sharla." *And at one time she'd believed him to be the right man for her.* "You'll get permanent custody of Sharla. Mark my words."

"I wish I could be as certain as you are."

Josie grinned. "Oh, it's easy to know what's best for someone else's life. It's when it comes to my own life that I can't see past my nose."

"At least you've got a long nose," he said. Michael casually reached out and touched the tip of her nose with his index finger, implying an intimacy she'd never felt with anyone else but him.

As she gently pushed his hand away, she caught his finger for a brief moment. The desire to entwine her fingers with his surprised her, even scared her. Being on her own for so long, she'd forgotten how comforting a man's touch could be. Swallowing hard, she acted as if his playful caress hadn't reached all the way to her heart.

They rode in silence for a few miles. Josie stole a glance at Michael's profile and wondered if he felt as unsettled as she did. But his countenance kept all his secrets.

"So what's going on in your own life that you can't get a handle on?" he asked. He braked the car, slowing as he exited the four-lane highway, and then turned right onto a narrow city street.

"Why do you ask that?" She hated that he seemed to see through her.

"You just said it's easier to know what's right for someone else than for yourself." Michael briefly glanced her way.

In an attempt to avoid his scrutiny, Josie looked out the window at the passing scenery. There'd been a time when wide-open space had marked the boundary between Tulsa and the suburbs. However, in the last few years both had spread, merging into one.

"I was talking in generalities, not specifics," she said.

"I don't buy that for a moment. I think you came home for a reason."

The understanding light in his eyes soothed her worried mind. Hadn't she been praying for someone to confide in? Was Michael the answer to her prayer? Or would it only bring her more trouble to share her concerns with him? The more entangled their lives became the more complex the engagement seemed to become.

She didn't have to tell him everything. And it would be such a relief to talk to someone. When she met his gaze, she understood why the children at school and church adored this man. Trust and compassion resided in his dark eyes. He put people at ease. He wore charisma like a perfectly fitted suit, and his sincerity drew people into his confidence. It drew her, too.

"You're right," she admitted. "I needed time off from work."

"I imagine work with the charity is exhausting." He spoke with the type of confidence that comes only with experience.

Though his work in the classroom and her work abroad differed, there were many similarities between their professions. Both thrived on the joy of watching children learn and mature, and both knew too well the emotional toll such work demanded.

"It's ironic," he continued. "Kids can fill your heart until it's about to bust, and yet, somehow in the same breath, they can drain every ounce of energy you have."

His perception amazed Josie. "Exactly. That's exactly how I feel. I'm empty inside."

"Coming home was a wise choice," he said.

Perhaps, but she had to wonder how wise it had been to agree to be his fiancée.

"I'm sure you could have gone anywhere for R and R."

She nodded. In the past, she'd chosen to vacation along the Mediterranean coast. But this time she'd needed more than sun, great food and relaxation. She'd needed to repair her soul, and for that there was no place better than home.

"I love my work, but I'm at a crossroads," she said, not certain which parts of her heart to reveal and which parts to keep hidden.

"And you're thinking it might be time for a change?" he prompted. He gripped the steering wheel tightly, as if the thought of her making a change might bother him.

"I might be forced to. The agency I work for is experiencing some financial problems, though it appears they're going to survive the setbacks of the past year."

"Still, nothing is ever certain."

"Exactly." The way he put her at ease made her want to open her heart and tell him everything. No one would understand how she felt about Angelina better than he. But she wasn't ready to share that side of her heart with him. Instead she said, "When I first learned the company might close, I was devastated. Then when things looked like they were getting back on track, I realized this was a good time for me to take stock of my life and reexamine the direction I was headed in."

"And your heart led you home?" His intense

gaze unnerved her. Without a doubt, she knew he would stare her down until she answered his question to his satisfaction.

"Yes, I followed my heart home." Josie swallowed hard, feeling as if she'd just admitted she'd been wrong to leave in the first place. She rushed past the uncomfortable thought. "I wanted to come home to a place where my faith seemed simple and uncomplicated."

Michael pushed one hand through his thick dark hair. With his focus on the street ahead, he said, "You can travel around the world and back again, but unless you're willing to honestly examine your heart, you won't find the answers you seek."

Josie nodded in order to avoid a potential argument, the conversation suddenly way too deep for her liking. No matter what Michael thought, she'd made the right choice seven years ago when she'd taken the job abroad. Through the charity organization, she'd had the privilege of providing food and medical services to children who wouldn't have survived without assistance. Every time she looked into a child's eyes she knew she'd been right to follow in Gran's footsteps. And with God's help, she would make new choices that were right for the future.

Seconds later, when Michael parked in front of a brick home, Josie silently thanked God for the reprieve. Confiding in Michael hadn't been a good idea after all.

Still seated in the car, Josie watched the front door

open and a small, barefoot girl race across the lawn. Michael rushed ahead with open arms, and Sharla jumped into them. The father and daughter hugged as if it'd been a month instead of a day since they'd last seen each other. And if there was any pain left from the car accident, Michael didn't show it. He hugged Sharla as if he were never going to let her go.

Josie remained in the car, allowing Sharla and Michael private time. Even with the window rolled down, she couldn't hear their voices clearly. With their heads bent toward each other, it was as if they communicated with their own special language. Sharla's mouth and hands moved in sync as she told her news. Then she opened her hand to reveal a hidden treasure, and Michael smiled as if she'd just shown him the Hope diamond. With eyes only for Michael, the young girl never even noticed Josie.

The resemblance between Sharla and Angelina amazed Josie and made her miss Angelina all the more. Had the two girls ever met, Josie had no doubt they would have been playmates. With their long dark hair, dark eyes and contagious laughter, the girls might even have been mistaken for sisters. But their lives were totally different.

Josie had found the orphaned Angelina living in a refugee camp. Though the scruffy child had been dirty and malnourished, there'd been a precious light in her doe eyes that had set her apart from the other children in the camp. Despite all the terrible things

Angelina had lived through, she hadn't given up on life. And it had been that spark of hope that had compelled Josie to fight for Angelina's life. But in the end, complications resulting from malnutrition had ended the little girl's life.

Josie wiped a tear from the corner of her eye. It had only been six months since Angelina's death, and yet this morning, it felt as if it had happened yesterday. She'd known better than to become so attached to the child, but when God sent an angel into your life it was impossible to turn your back— no matter what the cost might be. For that reason, she understood better than most why Michael would never stop fighting for Sharla. Just as she'd never stopped fighting for Angelina's health. Her efforts hadn't been near enough, and she prayed Michael wouldn't fail as she had. She hoped he would never know the unbearable pain such a loss brought.

When Michael looked her way and motioned her to join them, Josie inhaled deeply, then opened the car door. The instant Sharla noticed Josie, the girl's lean body stiffened and she took a step back, using Michael as her shield. Wary eyes proclaimed Josie an unwelcome intruder.

In an attempt to put Sharla at ease, Michael placed both hands on her shoulders and let Josie come to them.

"I would like you to meet an old friend, Josie Marshall. She's Mr. and Mrs. Marshall's daughter,''

Michael explained. "You remember Mrs. Marshall saying her daughter was coming home for a visit."

Sharla nodded shyly.

"You can do better than that," Michael prompted.

"Pleased to meet you, Miss Marshall," Sharla said, extending her hand as she'd obviously been taught. Though she looked at Josie, she carefully avoided meeting her gaze.

Josie bent down until she looked directly into the girl's solemn eyes. Grasping Sharla's hand, she said. "My friends call me Josie. And any friend of my mother's is a friend of mine."

"You have a nice mother," Sharla said. She relaxed her grip on Michael's arm with one hand, but let Josie continue to hold her other hand.

"You have beautiful hands," Josie remarked. "I especially love your purple nail polish. I bet it would look great on my nails." Josie held her free hand up for Sharla's scrutiny. She expected a giggle, but instead the young child's lip trembled.

"Grandma Rubee says I have my mother's hands." When Sharla's voice shook, Josie's heart broke.

With great tenderness, she turned Sharla's hand over and admired it from both sides. "How special you are to have your mother's hands. I have my mother's hands, too," Josie said.

"You do?" The idea seemed to intrigue Sharla.

"Yes, I do. And do you know that's a special

blessing from God?'' Josie hoped the thought might ease this child's pain.

Sharla shook her head.

''He did it so that when I'm far away from my mother, I can look at my hands and be reminded that she loves me and is praying for me.''

Sharla held both her hands out, turned them over, staring as if she were seeing them for the first time. ''Do you think my mom is praying for me?''

''Oh, Sharla, I do believe your mother is praying for you,'' Josie said, instinctively pulling the child close. Together they took a few steps to the front porch where Josie drew Sharla onto her lap and wrapped her arms around the girl. Nearby, Michael silently watched.

In her work, Josie had spent countless hours with motherless children. Though each child's needs were different, there were always common threads. Most experienced a deep need to be reassured that the love between mother and daughter still existed even though one had passed into God's realm. And most still needed to be mothered. Though no one could ever replace a mother's love, new arms were needed to provide love.

Sharla needed a mother as much as she needed a father.

The revelation rocked Josie. Was she really helping this child by working with Michael when her biological father offered both mother and father, as well as siblings? When she looked up and met Michael's eyes, she wondered if he could read her traitorous thoughts.

But as she held his gaze, her doubts melted away. Michael was this child's father in every sense of the word, and in time, he would marry and provide Sharla with the family security she deserved and needed.

Even before he moved, she sensed his need to be close to Sharla. Josie scooted to the right and Michael joined them. As if it were the most natural thing in the world, he slipped his arm around Sharla and Josie and held them both tight. Because he did this for Sharla, Josie didn't reject the embrace.

Protected by his arms and trapped in the overflow of his love, it was impossible not to pretend they were a family. For just a moment. But not any longer, because such thoughts were dangerous. They made Josie long for things she could never have with Michael.

Michael pressed his lips against the top of Sharla's head, inhaling the sweet scent of her hair. In minutes, Josie had been able to comfort Sharla in a way no one else had been able to. For that, he would always be grateful. But he had been wrong to bring her here.

He'd known that as soon as he'd slipped his arms around her and Sharla. Instantly, he'd forgotten the past and his heart had beat as if they were a family. The bittersweet moment angered him. This is what it could have been like, he thought.

Yet, he let the anger slip through his fingers. How could he stay mad at a woman who'd selflessly reached out to comfort a child? He'd never seen this side of Josie. He'd never seen her heal a child's wounds. All these years, he'd been angry at her and God, so certain she'd made the wrong choice in leaving him. For the first time, he glimpsed their lives from God's vantage point. Who was he to hold her back from the calling God had placed on her life?

When Sharla broke free of the embrace to chase after her calico cat, she left Josie and Michael in each other's awkward arms. Both pulled away quickly, grateful they could shift their attention to Sharla and the frisky cat.

"When you see her running and playing, it's hard to remember how much pain she's in." Michael continued to focus on Sharla, tensing up when she ran toward the street and relaxing when she and the cat plopped down in the middle of the yard and began to roll across the grass.

"I know," Josie said. "And even though she misses her mother, I can tell you've been there for her. With your love, she's going to be all right." Josie, too, let her gaze linger on the energetic child.

"Where'd you learn to do this?"

Her brows arched together and her eyes narrowed. "Do what?"

"Comfort a girl you'd never met?"

"I don't know that what I did took any special

skill. I was just willing to love a child who needed me.''

Michael looked down at his hands. The incident only served to remind him that when he gained custody of Sharla he would be both mother and father to this child. And Sharla needed a mother.

Until Denise's death, Michael had been willing to patiently wait for the right woman to come along. But on the day he'd accepted responsibility for Sharla his prayers for a wife had increased a hundredfold. He trusted God to send them a special woman.

But it wasn't Josie they needed. She might be good in a pinch, but she wasn't the kind of woman you could count on to stay. She'd left him before, and she would leave him again.

Still, it was ironic that Josie was the only woman Sharla had responded to other than Grandma Rubee. Several women from the church had reached out to Sharla, but the dark-eyed girl had recoiled each time. It was for Sharla's sake, he told himself, that he wouldn't risk any more visits between his daughter and former girlfriend. The child's heart was too fragile to risk being broken again.

Sharla started doing cartwheels around the cat, and Josie jumped up and joined in. Around and around they rotated, rubbery arms and legs sailing through the air, until they both collapsed with dizziness. Lying on the ground they laughed hysterically as Michael and the cat eyed them suspiciously.

The morning passed quickly as Sharla filled the

silence with her endless chatter. They stopped at the mall first, where Sharla bought a present for the birthday party she would attend later that afternoon, as well as new summer clothes. Next, they ran errands for Grandma Rubee, picking up a prescription and several grocery items. After lunch at the restaurant of Sharla's choice, they said goodbye.

Josie went ahead to the car so Sharla and Michael could share a private moment. Just as she opened the door, she felt the tug on the back of her shirt. Turning to face Sharla, the child gave her a big hug, and then before Josie could say a word, Sharla ran for the house and disappeared inside.

The silent hug spoke volumes, and warmed Josie's heart in a way she hadn't expected. While she would always miss Angelina, these few hours with Sharla had eased her pain in ways hours of introspection and prayer had failed.

"A penny for your thoughts," Michael said.

Jarred back to the present, Josie got into the car. "I was thinking I'd just been with an angel."

Michael's face reddened as if he were offended. He started the car and jerked it into gear. Josie wondered how he could have misinterpreted her compliment.

"You understand you won't be seeing her again." Michael turned to look at her to ensure there was no misunderstanding.

Josie nodded, the moment becoming clearer. Her easy rapport with Sharla had threatened him. But that still didn't make sense. Surely he knew she wouldn't do anything to hurt the girl. He could only feel threatened if he still cared about Josie.

Michael shifted his focus back to the road, his lips and brows tight with tension. Josie continued to study his angular profile, hoping for yet another sign to confirm what she could hardly believe. Michael still cared for her. He might even still love her.

Josie took a deep breath and swallowed hard. Yes, they both still cared for each other. How could they not? Having grown up together and then being first loves it was only natural they felt connected. But you couldn't build a future on the kind of love they felt. They were old friends. Nothing more. Well, maybe a little more.

Chapter Seven

"Josie, Michael…do you have a minute?"

Josie figured her mother must have been watching for her and Michael to return. No sooner had they parked the car at Michael's, than her mother called out to them from the Marshalls' back porch.

Michael looked at Josie and shrugged his shoulders as if to say it would be useless to avoid her mother. Eventually, she would track them down.

"I've made iced tea and chocolate chip cookies," she said.

"Sounds great, Mom," Josie called out. "You will join us won't you?" The drive home in silence had almost been more than she could endure.

"For a few minutes. Actually, there is something I would like to discuss with you."

Josie and Michael stole another glance. Michael mouthed the words, *wedding plans,* and within seconds, the challenge of diverting Mrs. Marshall's attention united them.

By the time they reached the house, Sarah had already poured the iced tea into two tall glasses, which sat side by side on the wicker coffee table. Josie and Michael each took a glass, then moved to chairs at opposite ends of the small, enclosed patio. Josie immediately noticed the stack of brides' magazines, but didn't comment.

"How did your visit go?" Mrs. Marshall asked.

"Very nice," Josie said. "Sharla's a wonderful child. We hit it off instantly."

"I'm so glad. But I can't say I'm surprised. I knew you two would love each other."

Michael nervously set his glass of tea down, sloshing a bit over the edge. "We haven't told Sharla about our engagement. We didn't think it would be wise until she knows Josie a little better. She's been through so much."

Mrs. Marshall considered Michael's decision for a moment, then added, "You're right to wait. But I predict she's going to be thrilled when you tell her. As thrilled as I am. You know," she said, looking at Josie, "you're making me a grandmother."

Josie swallowed so hard she thought she might never find her voice again.

"A grandmother," she repeated.

"Technically, she'll be my stepgrandchild, but that won't matter to your father and me. We already love her dearly. You know we'll treat her as if she were your own. You aren't worried about that are you, dear?''

Josie shook her head. Sarah Marshall had enough love for all the children in the world and then some. "The thought never crossed my mind."

Thankfully, Michael came to the rescue and redirected the conversation. "You needed to talk to us about something?"

"Now you know I would never barge in where it wasn't my business—"

Josie quickly interrupted. "We know that, Mom."

Though that was exactly what Sarah was doing. Josie had no doubt that given the chance her mother would plan the wedding right down to the smallest detail. And love every minute of the process.

"Judy called me this afternoon, and she started telling me about her daughter's wedding. You do remember Judy and her daughter, Lindsay?"

Josie nodded. For as long as she could remember, Judy had been her mother's closest friend. Though Lindsay and Josie had been playmates as children, they hadn't hung out together in high school due to a two-year age difference. When Michael fidgeted in his seat, Josie recalled he had dated Lindsay within the last year. As she'd read the news in her mother's letter, she'd known Lindsay wasn't right for him. In fact, she couldn't see Michael with anyone but...now where had that thought come from? Josie wondered, as she tried to refocus her attention on her mother.

"Anyway, Lindsay has found a fabulous wedding coordinator. I hope you don't mind, but I went ahead and left a message for her. I'm keeping my fingers crossed she'll be able to work with us."

"Oh, Mom," Josie said. "You didn't tell Judy we were getting married did you?"

"When have I ever broken my word?" Sarah asked. "Of course, I didn't tell her. Though I was tempted. This is such great news. I don't understand why—"

Michael cast Josie a loving gaze that would have melted her heart had she not known it was for show. "Mrs. Marshall," he began.

"Call me Mom. After all, we're going to be family soon."

Michael smiled. "All right, Mom. Try to understand that Josie and I want some quiet time to ourselves before we make the announcement."

"Well, Judy and my other friends are going to be upset when they learn I've been holding out on them."

"I think they'll understand," Josie said.

"Well, I just hope I don't let the cat out of the bag."

Josie prayed her mother would never discover their engagement was merely make-believe. It would deeply hurt her to learn she'd been deceived. Even if it was for a good cause.

Compelled to do some damage control, Josie tried to soften the coming blow. "Mom, try to see this from our viewpoint. We've already been engaged once and it didn't work. We're scared. We don't want a lot of outside pressure until we sort some things out for ourselves.''

Sarah narrowed her eyes and bit down on her lip. ''Michael,'' she said, looking directly at him with her best mother-in-law gaze, ''do you love my daughter?''

Michael glanced down at his clasped hands, and when he looked up, meeting Josie's gaze, she lost her breath. If she hadn't known he was pretending, she would have sworn he cared for her in the way a man loves his wife. ''Yes, I love your daughter.''

Turning toward Josie, Sarah said, ''And do you love Michael?''

Without hesitation, Josie said, ''Yes, I love Michael.''

But not like you think, Mom, she silently added. I love him because he is part of my past. I will always care about him, but I don't love him in the way a woman should love her husband.

''What more do you need?'' Sarah said. ''You love each other, and I've always known you were meant to be. I knew it the first time I saw you together.''

This time, the amused smile that passed between Michael and Josie was for real. Sarah loved this story, and she told it often and to whoever would listen.

Josie no longer knew if the moment remained so

clear in her mind because she remembered that first meeting or because her mother had told the story so many times. Either way, a five-year-old Josie had fallen off of her new bike and landed facedown in the gravel driveway. Through the hedge archway, Michael had seen her fall, and he'd come running so hard he'd tripped over his feet and had landed on top of her. By the time Sarah arrived, Michael had pulled Josie free of the bike and was wiping her tears with his chubby hands, telling her she would be okay if she would just quit crying.

"Mom, can you give us a few more days?" Josie asked.

"If you insist," Sarah said, and when she smiled Josie knew her mother would do anything in the world for her.

Overcome with love, Josie jumped up and threw her arms around Sarah and said, "You're the best."

Sarah immediately reached out for Michael, and once again Josie found herself in a family embrace. There was no place in the world more secure than in her mother's arms. And in Michael's.

Josie pulled away first. "This wedding-planning business is turning me into a sentimental fool," she joked in an attempt to conceal her vulnerable heart.

"From what I hear, a person needs a great sense of humor to get through an engagement," Michael said.

"Oh, men," Josie and her mother chimed in unison.

"I'm definitely outnumbered," Michael said, standing as if he were going to leave.

"Not for long," Sarah said. "I need to take Gran to the grocery store. I'll be back in an hour. Make sure those cookies are gone before I return."

Michael stayed put until Sarah had left in the car. And even then he lingered, finishing his iced tea and eating one more cookie.

As if he were suddenly aware of her curious gaze, Michael said, "What?"

"Nothing," Josie replied, as she wrestled with her thoughts.

"There's obviously something on your mind. What is it?"

Josie bit her bottom lip, debating whether to confide in him. There'd been a time when she could have said anything to this man and known how he would have responded. But she didn't know this Michael in that way. She might be about to open a Pandora's box that should remain locked.

"Well?" Michael prodded. Her vagueness had intrigued him, and he wasn't going to let her off the hook.

"I was merely thinking about how much things have changed since I left home. And especially how much we've both changed." Because she seemed to have his attention, she continued. "I look at you, and you seem like the man I once knew. You're handsome as ever." Michael's eyes sparkled with pleasure at the honest admission. "You have so many of the same mannerisms—like the way you push your hands through your hair when you're frustrated, or the way you tap your foot when you're nervous and the way you blush when my mother embarrasses you. But—"

"But I'm not the same man you knew," he finished her sentence.

"No…and I guess I'm not the same woman you knew, either."

Michael stared off across the back lawn as if the explanation for these changes clung to the soft yellow roses that climbed the arbor Josie's father had built. When he turned toward her again the bitter anger lighting his eyes surprised her.

"When the girl you think you're going to spend the rest of your life with runs off to save the world, you can't help but change." Michael gripped the chair arm so tightly she heard the wicker pop.

Josie jerked back, raising her hand to her face. Her cheek stung as if he'd slapped her. Truth lurked in his hurtful words, but not the whole truth.

"You didn't even try to stop me," she said, her voice rising in both pitch and volume.

"Would it have made any difference?" he asked, his eyes locked on hers.

"We'll never know, will we?" Josie's heart beat so hard and fast she feared it would explode in her chest.

"Oh, Josie," Michael exclaimed, briefly covering his face with his hands. "I didn't want you if I had to beg you to stay. In the long run, where would that have gotten us? If I had begged, and if you'd stayed, the day would have come when you would have resented me for denying your dreams.''

''Who made you God?'' she asked, angered by his certainty of what the future would have held for them. How could he have read her so wrong? If he had only asked, she would have stayed. She turned away from him, remembering the pain she'd felt when they'd broken up, and reliving it all over again.

Gathering her courage, she faced him. ''I always thought we belonged together. Even the day I left Tulsa, I thought our love would draw us close again. But I was wrong. Maybe what happened was for the best. We proved our love wasn't the forever kind of love.''

Michael shrugged his shoulders. ''We were young, Josie. We thought we knew about love and life, but we didn't know anything about living in the real world.''

''We could have learned together.'' Josie crossed her arms over her chest and hugged herself to ward off the pain.

''You had big dreams. You still do. And after watching you comfort Sharla, I have no doubt you're doing the work God intended for you to do.''

''You're more certain than I am.''

''Why do you say that?'' Curiosity misted his dark eyes.

''What would you think if I told you I was thinking about making a career change? Maybe even coming back to Tulsa?'' Josie held her breath, afraid his response might hurt more than she could bear.

Michael inhaled deeply, then paced to the far side of the porch. It was as if he didn't dare stay close for fear he might fall under her spell again.

''I'd say decisions scare you,'' he challenged.

His answer wasn't at all what she'd expected. ''That's not true. I make decisions all the time.''

''I'm talking about the really big decisions. Like the one you say you've come home to Tulsa to make. We both know you're going back to London.''

''How can you be so certain?'' She squeezed her hands into a tight fist in order to control her frustration.

Michael stopped pacing directly in front of her. He pushed his hands through his hair and grimaced. ''Because I know you. You don't make decisions. You don't like change. You let circumstances dictate your life.''

''That's a really harsh thing to say.'' She didn't have to listen to his insults, she told herself. She could walk away now. What did he really know about her life anyway? But an inner voice urged her to at least listen to what Michael had to say.

Michael pushed his hands into his pockets, suddenly reluctant to speak. ''I don't see how this is doing us any good.''

Josie crossed to him quickly, and placing a hand

on his arm said, "Please stay. I would really like to hear your opinion."

She'd always valued Michael's insight, and in the past he'd never intentionally hurt her. Seeing herself from his perspective might help her resolve the turmoil in her heart. No matter how much it hurt.

"Remember, you asked for my opinion." Michael refilled his iced tea glass, then took a long, slow sip. "You're always looking for the green light, Josie. You believe everything is a sign from God."

"What do you mean?"

Michael swallowed hard, as if it were difficult to put his thoughts into words. "After high school, you couldn't decide which college to attend. But as soon as I made my choice, you followed."

"What was wrong with that? I thought you wanted us to be together."

"I did," he admitted. "But that's not my point. You didn't really make a decision. You hitched a ride on my dream. And after college graduation, you sent out dozens of résumés and then you accepted the first job offer. You didn't even make a decision about us. You just left, and when I didn't chase after you, you decided we weren't meant to be. Do you see a pattern here?"

Josie met Michael's intense gaze briefly, and then looked down at her feet, at the platter of half eaten cookies, at the birdbath in the lawn, anywhere to avoid the truth in Michael's eyes.

She opened her mouth to deny his claims, but

nothing came out. Could he be right? Did she really let circumstances dictate her life?

Just as she started to admit he might be right, Michael grabbed her by the upper arms and asked, "Josie, are you ever going to take charge of your life and go after what God desires for you?"

Shaking her head, Josie backed away from his reach. She needed time to pray about what he'd said. Not wanting him to see how deeply his accusations had shaken her, she instinctively protected her heart. With as much confidence as she could muster, she said, "I have taken charge of my life. My work with children is exactly what God has called me to do."

Not waiting for his response, Josie slipped into the house and shut the door. Leaning against the wall, hot tears raced down her face.

Michael was right. The fear of making the wrong choice petrified her, and at the cornerstone of her fear resided a lack of faith and trust in God.

The vicious circle trapped her like a hamster running on an exercise wheel. Without trust and faith, change seemed impossible. And though the work she did with children was good, if she continued with the status quo she might be missing God's real purpose for her life.

"Calm down," Josie whispered to herself.

When she'd come home, she hadn't expected the answers to be easy or simple, nor had she expected to work her problems out overnight.

One thing, though, had become very clear to her

in the two weeks she'd been home. There were no second chances with Michael. The choice she'd made seven years ago was irreversible. In a few weeks, she would leave Tulsa—and Michael—again. Why this troubled her heart, she didn't understand.

Michael worked throughout the afternoon and into the night on Sharla's playhouse, eager for it to be finished by the time the court awarded him custody.

But tonight as he sawed lumber and pounded nails, he didn't think of the little girl. Instead, his thoughts centered on Josie. With every strike of the hammer he tried to erase her image from his mind.

But he failed.

The distressed look on her face just before she'd slipped into the house haunted him. He shouldn't have been so harsh. Who was he to judge her, anyway?

His motivation had been selfish. He hadn't wanted to help her as much as he'd wanted to hurt her, to lash out at her for letting go of their love. And he'd wanted to protect himself from her. She'd only been home a short time, and already, little by little, he felt their lives becoming entangled.

Sitting down on an overturned bucket, he covered his face with this hands. The whole day had been a disaster, from Sharla's fondness for Josie to Sarah Marshall forcing him to say he loved her daughter.

What had he gotten himself into?

Then, as if he sensed her presence, Michael

looked up in time to see a shadow flee Josie's bedroom window. The fact that he'd known she watched him disturbed him more than her nearness.

Determined to clear his mind of Josie, Michael picked up the hammer and swung hard. With two clean strokes the nail pierced the wood. Stepping back, Michael admired his handiwork. Even in this unfinished stage, the playhouse promised to deliver hours of girlish dreaming and delight.

"Wow, this fairy-tale castle is really something."

Though the deep voice startled Michael, he immediately recognized Eddie. What a way to end the day, he thought.

"What can I do for you?" Michael asked. He clutched the hammer tightly.

"I hoped you would see it that way." Eddie circled around Michael, keeping a wide berth as he walked toward the playhouse and entered the stud structure. His boots echoed on the plywood floor. "Sharla said the playhouse was spectacular, and I've got to agree with her."

Michael didn't like the way Eddie had barged in, but he promised himself he would keep his cool. Gritting his teeth, he counted to ten under his breath. Sparring with Sharla's biological father wouldn't win him any points with the court. And more importantly, it wouldn't help Sharla.

"Anne Devon came to see me today," Eddie said. "She had a little news. Said you were engaged."

"That's right." Michael volunteered no more information than necessary. His attorney had warned him not to talk to Eddie outside of court.

"A little fast, isn't it?" Eddie wore the confidence of a man who believed checkmate was only one move away.

Michael wanted to say his engagement wasn't any of Eddie's business, but whatever affected either man, impacted Sharla. "Josie and I have been together since high school," Michael said, skipping over their seven-year separation. "She's been working abroad, and when she came home two weeks ago we decided we didn't want to wait any longer."

"You really think a judge is going to buy that story?" Eddie asked.

"It's the truth." Michael nudged a piece of scrap wood with his toe. Deception made him uncomfortable. How many times had he cautioned his Sunday school class that telling half-truths was akin to lying? Yet, he spun this truth to suit his own purposes. Everything he did, he did for Sharla, he told himself, convinced that somehow in the end winning custody of the girl would make it all right.

"Well, regardless of the truth, I came here to make you an offer."

Though Eddie spoke as though he held the upper hand, Michael noticed the beads of sweat clinging to the man's receding hairline.

"What offer is that?"

"For Sharla's sake, let's settle this between us. How can a court know what's best for my girl?"

Michael didn't answer the rhetorical question, but waited patiently to hear the proposal.

"I'll get straight to the matter. If you'll agree that Sharla should live with me, my wife and our two children, then I'll make certain you have liberal visitation rights."

"You would do that?" Michael said, as if he were seriously considering the idea.

"Sure. I want what's best for my little girl. I want her to have a home with a full-time mom and to grow up with her stepbrother and stepsister."

Michael bit down on his lip, reminding himself of his promise to stay calm, cool and collected.

"She can have all that with me," Michael countered.

Eddie shook his head. "I don't see how. It's pretty tough on a family when the mother works halfway around the world. And surely you don't want to tear Sharla from the life she's known and drag her to a foreign country."

"Tear her from the life she's always known?" Michael echoed.

Again, he felt Josie's presence before she approached from behind and intimately slipped her arm around his waist.

"Don't get your hopes up thinking you can paint a bleak scenario for the judge. Michael and I have no intentions of uprooting Sharla. She's been through too much already. And as for a family, we can give her that, too."

The color drained from Eddie's face when Josie spoke. Michael nearly choked on air at the thought of Josie pregnant with his child. Instantly, an old image flashed through his mind. On a hot, summer night, they'd cuddled on the front porch swing. "Once we're married, I don't think we should wait to have children," Josie had said. Michael, too full of love and hope to answer, had merely squeezed her tightly.

"If you don't want to uproot Sharla, then the logical and the compassionate thing to do would be to leave her with me. I'm the only father she's ever known." Raw emotion wedged in Michael's throat making speaking difficult.

As if she'd read his mind, Josie finished his thoughts. "Michael has been there for Sharla from the beginning. He made sure Denise had excellent prenatal care. He coached Denise through labor and held Sharla seconds after she entered the world. He walked the floor with her when she cried and he held her tight, letting her know that as long as she was with him she was safe and loved. Now, I don't know where you were during those times, but you weren't with your daughter."

Michael regained control of his voice, and said, "I don't deny Sharla needs you in her life. She needs to know her biological father and siblings. But I'm her anchor. Please don't take that away from her. Not after all she's been through."

Eddie pulled his car keys from his pocket and jangled them between his fingers. "I'd hoped you would be reasonable about this. I can see we don't have any choice but to let the judge decide."

Michael bit his tongue to keep from shouting that he had a letter Denise had written after the court had appointed Michael Sharla's legal guardian. The letter, written from her heart just before her death, revealed her most private wishes for her daughter's future. Denise had even provided for the possibility that Eddie might someday desire a relationship with his daughter. In fact, she'd prayed Eddie would come looking for Sharla one day, but even so, she wanted Michael to raise her daughter.

And the real ace was the second letter no one, not even his lawyer, had ever seen. The one Denise had written to Josie. Countless times, she'd told Michael he'd been a fool to let Josie get away. She'd never stopped believing Michael and Josie belonged together. And on the chance Michael would someday wise up, she wanted Josie to raise her daughter.

"I think we'd better leave this to the court," Michael said, confident the momentum was on his side.

Eddie started to leave, and then he walked back. "I'll believe this engagement is for real when I see a ring on her finger."

Chapter Eight

"Thanks for coming over," Michael said. "I think it helped for Eddie to see us together. He was so certain we were pretending to be engaged he thought he could bluff me into giving up my fight for Sharla."

"Just playing my role," Josie said. Seeming as uncomfortable as he felt, she turned to leave.

Michael gathered up his tools and deposited them in an empty five-gallon bucket, then carried them to the garage.

"Josie. Wait," he called out as she passed by. Clasping her hand, he pulled her close. "I want to apologize for the way I spoke to you this afternoon. I had no right."

Josie shrugged her shoulders, understanding he wasn't apologizing for what he'd said, just how he'd said it. "I asked for your opinion. I'm a big girl. I can handle honesty."

"Even so, what right do I have to judge you? We hardly know each other anymore. There's so much about your life I don't know."

An outdoor light came on automatically, warding off the approaching darkness. Standing in the spotlight, Josie felt as if she and Michael were caught in their own private play. Act One had been their first engagement. Act Two had opened with their pretend engagement. And where would Act Three leave them?

When she returned to work would they keep in contact? Would they e-mail and talk on the telephone occasionally? Or would they simply drift apart again? This time for good. If she was forced to predict, she would have to choose the latter. Unless something changed between her and Michael, continuing a casual friendship would be too awkward and difficult.

Yet, she couldn't imagine her life without him as her friend. She had no doubt God had called her home at this time. But maybe this trip wasn't just about bolstering her wavering faith. Maybe it was about making amends with Michael. Maybe she needed to go back and heal a past wound before God would allow her to move in a new direction.

"Your apology means a lot to me," Josie said. "And for the record, what you said was right on the mark. Perhaps you know me better than you think you do.''

With a tender touch, Michael brushed an errant strand of hair from her forehead and hooked it around her ear. Josie swallowed hard, as her pulse quickened. Nonchalantly, she wiped her sweaty palms on her thighs.

Meeting his gaze, she dared to say, ''Being with you is confusing. I can't separate the Michael I once loved from the man you've become.''

''I'm not so different,'' he claimed. His steady gaze made her feel as if she were the only woman in the world.

''Yes, you are,'' she insisted. ''You know where you're going now and what you want, and that has changed you.''

''Maybe not all for the better.'' When his eyes turned somber, she realized something troubled him.

''Are you telling me you've got a deep dark secret?'' she teased.

The seriousness faded, replaced by amusement. ''Don't we all?''

''Yeah, I suppose we do.'' Josie instantly thought of Angelina.

Silence fell between them like a theater curtain. But for the first time, it wasn't uncomfortable. They didn't have to reveal details to know they'd both lived through hard times which had shaken and molded their characters, as well as forcing them to grow up.

In an attempt to heal the wounds from the past, Josie took the first step. "I'm sorry about the way I left you seven years ago. I didn't handle it very well. And I hope you will forgive my youthful ignorance. I really did love you, and I never meant to hurt you." *And she'd never meant to cut him out of her life.*

Michael took a deep breath and exhaled loudly. He softly brushed the back of his hand across her cheek, down her jawbone, and under her chin. "I'm sorry, too. I was just as young and ignorant. And just as afraid of commitment as you were." Then in a very low voice he added, "And I loved you, too."

They gazed at each other without flinching, as if they were afraid to look away and break the magic.

Finally, Josie spoke. "We were afraid of commitment. I hadn't thought of it in that way." But the more she did, the more it made sense. And commitment still frightened her because she knew from losing Angelina and Michael's love how much it hurt when you were forced to let go of someone. She never wanted to feel that kind of pain again.

"Do you think we can be friends?" Josie asked.

"I don't know. I'm willing to try if you are."

Josie extended her hand, and Michael covered it with his. Pulling her fingers to his lips, he kissed her palm.

"Breakfast is ready," Sarah called from the bottom of the stairway.

Still dressed in her bathrobe, Josie staggered to the top of the stairs. "I'm not feeling well," she said. At least not well enough to risk walking into church with her mother. Sarah wanted so desperately to announce the engagement to her friends that the good news was bound to burst forth from her lips. "I thought I would sleep in this morning."

Sarah hurried up the stairs, as if this were a life-and-death situation. Pressing her hand against Josie's forehead, she said, "You don't have a fever, your color is good, and your eyes are clear."

"I'm okay. It's just a headache," Josie assured her.

Sarah wiped her hands on her apron. "I know you think I'm overreacting."

"You are, but it's okay. You know I worry about you, too."

Sarah cocked her head in amazement. "Whatever for?"

"I'm worried you've taken on too much. Especially now that Gran is getting older and needs you more."

"I'll be the first to admit things get busy at times, but it's nothing I can't handle."

"Hey, us Marshall women are strong," Josie said, uncomfortable with where the conversation was destined to end. She'd given her mother the perfect opening to suggest she come home permanently. With Josie in Tulsa, Sarah would know her daughter was safe from the hazards of working in third-world countries and Josie could help her mother with Gran.

Josie crawled back into bed, and Sarah tucked in the sheet, then sat on the edge of the mattress.

"Is there trouble between you and Michael?" she asked.

"Mother," Josie said. How like her to go right to the point. "No. Why would you think that?"

Sarah shrugged her shoulders. "Oh, it's nothing I can put my finger on. When you're together, it's like you're a couple that's not quite in sync."

At a complete loss as to how she should answer, Josie stalled for time by scratching the side of her neck.

"I don't know what you're talking about." But she did know that if she and Michael couldn't convince her mother they were in love, then they couldn't hope to convince the caseworker.

"Your father says it's none of my business."

Josie yawned and stretched, crowding her mother closer to the edge of the bed in the hopes she would take the gentle hint to leave.

Sarah stood, but kept her back to the door. "I've always believed you and Michael belonged together. I don't want anything to go wrong."

"We need time," Josie said. "We've been apart. We've got some catching up to do."

"Are you sure that's all?"

"I'm positive. We've both changed, and we're getting to know our new and improved selves."

Sarah pursed her lips as she considered the claim. "From what I see, you're pretty much the same people. A little older. A little wiser. And even more in love than before."

Thinking quickly, Josie added, "But it takes more than love to make a relationship work."

Sarah clapped her hands loudly and smiled. "Isn't that the truth."

Josie grinned at her mother's exuberance.

Sarah glanced at Josie's alarm clock. "Now, it looks to me like that headache of yours has gone with the wind. You've still got time for a shower and a quick breakfast before we leave for church. I've already asked Michael to ride with us."

In protest, Josie pulled the covers over her head. She should have known she couldn't outsmart her mother.

Popping back out, she said, "Mom, promise me you won't announce our engagement today."

Sarah just smiled, withholding the reassuring words Josie longed to hear.

Josie and Michael walked up the stone church steps behind her parents. Old friends greeted her with waves, smiles and friendly handshakes. When her family passed through the thick, wooden doors, she felt the curious stares follow. Though her mother had kept her word and hadn't breathed a word about the engagement, it was obvious the whole church knew Michael and Josie were spending a lot of time together.

"Excuse me," Josie said to Michael and her parents. "I see an old friend from high school I want to say hello to."

Uncomfortable being on display, Josie put as much distance between herself and Michael as possible. While it was necessary for people to think they were a couple, she desperately hoped to avoid well-meaning comments. *We're so happy to see you together again. Is there any news we should know about? We always thought you were the perfect couple.*

Crossing the spacious entryway, she called out to the woman holding a newborn infant. "Stephanie."

Stephanie looked up and smiled, then with her free arm gave Josie a huge hug. "I'd heard you were home. You look fabulous."

"Thanks, so do you." Less than three months after the birth of her second child, Stephanie already looked trim. But it was the sparkle of motherhood in her eyes that made her beautiful.

"You're too kind," Stephanie quipped. "But I'll take the compliment. My mother-in-law spent the night, so I got a full eight hours' rest for once. Trust me, uninterrupted sleep cures the dark circles under the eyes."

"It's just so good to see you," Josie said, eager to bombard her friend with a hundred questions. "I was hoping to drop by and visit with you."

Stephanie had been Josie's best friend throughout high school. Back then they'd never dreamed life would take them in different directions and they would lose contact. Only recently, on Josie's last trip home for her parents' anniversary party had they reconnected. Much to their surprise and joy, they picked up their friendship as if the quiet years between them had never existed.

"If you can't find the time, I'll understand." A mischievous smile burst across Stephanie's face.

"Of course, I have time," Josie said. Then she turned to follow Stephanie's gaze and found it directed toward Michael.

His tailored suit hung perfectly over his lean body. With his dark, wavy hair brushed back, he projected an air of confidence and dependability. He looked mature, but not stuffy. Lurking beneath the polished exterior she sensed a man who loved adventure and wasn't afraid of passion. If she'd never met him before, she would have quietly asked around until she learned his name, his occupation and if he was unattached, because he looked exactly like the man she'd been dreaming of spending the rest of her life with.

Josie blinked twice and swallowed hard. This is Michael, she reminded herself, surfacing from the disturbing thoughts.

"From what I hear you don't have much time," Stephanie said, shifting the weight of the sleepy baby from one arm to the other.

"And exactly what have you heard?" She extended her arms, and Stephanie tenderly trusted her daughter to Josie's embrace.

"Rumor is you and Michael are a hot item. You've been seen all over town together. You're affectionate, and though your mother won't confirm the news, we all think love is in the air."

"We're old friends," Josie protested. But the look in Stephanie's eyes told her she wasn't buying the act.

"You might be friends, but you're also a lot more."

"All right," Josie confided. "We're going to see what happens."

Stephanie suddenly turned serious. "Be careful. It's not just you and Michael this time. There's a child involved."

"You know Sharla?" Josie asked.

"She was in the Sunday school class I taught last year. She's a wonderful girl. And while she may seem tough on the outside, her heart is fragile."

Josie nodded. "I wouldn't do anything to hurt her."

Stephanie's smile waned. "Good intentions aren't enough."

From another person, the warning might have offended Josie, but she knew her friend's heart. "We're being really careful around Sharla. That's one of the reasons we're keeping a low profile. We don't want to get her hopes up."

Stephanie rubbed the top of her daughter's head. "You're going to love being a mother."

"She's going to be a wonderful mother," Michael said, joining the two women. When he offered one finger to the infant, she instantly wrapped her tiny fingers around his. "She's beautiful."

Josie looked at Michael and marveled at the hunger in his eyes. He wanted to be a father and a husband. Suddenly, she felt as if she were looking at what her life would have been like if she'd stayed in Tulsa. She and Michael would have married, and they would have had two or three children, maybe even more.

Stephanie reached for her baby, and as Josie gave back the infant, she relinquished the dream. What more evidence did she need to prove that God had brought her home to sever her ties with Michael? Giving up the past seemed easy compared to letting go of the what-could-have-been. Rationally, she'd known her relationship with Michael had ended when she'd taken the overseas job. Apparently, her heart still harbored hope.

Michael leaned close to her ear and said, "Your parents and Gran are ready to go in." Anyone watching would have thought he whispered loving endearments.

Josie made the mistake of looking at him. She saw the kiss coming, but she couldn't turn away in time. Or maybe she didn't want to turn away. His lips pressed against hers briefly in a way that said *we belong together,* then taking her arm he escorted her into the sanctuary.

Heads turned as Josie and Michael passed through the doorway. On the way down the aisle, the "Wedding March" blared in her head. She managed to squelch the internal music, only to have it replaced with images of white roses, Venetian lace, silk organza and pearls. One day her father would walk her down this aisle to the love of her life.

Somehow, Josie managed to find her seat without tripping or losing her balance. With great restraint, she resisted glancing at Michael every few seconds. What on earth had possessed him to kiss her in front of everyone? Friendly rumors already had them headed for the altar.

Josie glanced at her mother. Sarah sported a smile that could have illuminated New York City during a blackout. Oh great, Josie thought, convinced Michael had just given her mother the green light to move ahead with the wedding plans.

The music director raised her arms, and the congregation began to sing. Josie flipped through the hymnal, but the numbers were blurred. Determined to find the hymn, she kept searching, nearly tearing the pages out of the hymnal. Then Michael calmly returned her book to the pew and shared his with her. Their hands barely touched as they both grasped the book near the center binding. He pointed to the beginning of the second verse. She opened her mouth to sing, but nothing came out. His closeness disturbed her more than she wanted to admit.

The announcements, prayers, scripture readings and sermon flew by without Josie hearing a coherent word. At a time when she should have been worshipping God and seeking His direction for her life, her thoughts centered on the man sitting next to her.

The longer she sat by him, the more old memories taunted her. She recalled an afternoon when they'd sat by the lake and planned their wedding. Another time, they'd described the house they would build. Once, they'd even picked names for their children.

Michael's relaxed smile and concentration on the service troubled her the most. How could he kiss her and act as if nothing had happened? Why didn't he remember how good their love had been?

Josie looked at her watch and wondered if time could possibly pass more slowly. Impatient to distance herself from Michael and all the smug looks, she broke out in a sweat. If she didn't get out of here soon, she would explode. Somewhere between the time she'd entered the church and the time she'd sat down, the line separating the pretend from the real world had blurred into one.

Finally, the minister said Amen and the congregation dispersed. With one hand on Josie's shoulder, Sarah said, "I think it's time we planned an engagement party."

Josie groaned.

If she possessed any sense, she would be on the next flight to London.

. . . .

Chapter Nine

Michael watched the rain hit the windows hard and
slide down the smooth glass as if it fell in sheets
instead of drops. Barely past noon, streetlights
glowed in the premature darkness while streaks of
lightning flashed through the sky and lit the
drenched landscape. His hopes that the storm would
pass quickly diminished with each boom of thunder.

"So much for working on the playhouse," he
muttered, shoving his hands into his blue jeans pockets.

After spending the morning at the Tulsa Zoo with
Sharla, he'd planned to work the rest of the day on
the playhouse roof. Thanks to the generosity of a
fellow church member who'd recently replaced his
own roof, the playhouse would proudly sport fra-
grant cedar shingles.

Sharla had clapped her hands and jumped up and

down at the news. "It's going to be so cool," she'd exclaimed. "I'm the luckiest girl in Tulsa."

Tears had filled Michael's eyes. *And I'm the luckiest dad.*

The rain continued with no signs of tapering off. Since he couldn't work outside, Michael opted to get a head start on new ideas for next year's third-grade class.

His home office on the second floor had been his childhood bedroom. When he'd purchased the house from his parents five years ago, he'd believed he would be married with a family by now. His original remodeling plan called for this area to be a nursery. But as the years passed, it'd seemed silly to let the room remain idle. Plus, the empty space had become a painful reminder of what was missing in his life.

After booting up the computer, he checked his e-mail and did some research on the Internet. His concentration quickly waned, and he found his thoughts returning to the old dream.

He'd carefully mapped out his life. After college graduation, he'd planned to marry Josie. He would teach school, and she would find work with a children's agency in Tulsa. Within a year or two, they would start a family. They'd both agreed they wanted a full house. At least three, maybe four children, they'd said.

But the balloon had burst when Josie had accepted the job abroad, leaving him alone. Then Sharla had come into his life, and he'd thought that if he couldn't have his original dream, at least he could have a revised version. But now Eddie threatened that dream.

When the doorbell rang, Michael said a silent thank you for the interruption. Rushing down the stairs, he opened the door and looked directly at a very soggy Josie.

"Can I come in?" she asked.

"Sure, sure," Michael said, realizing he'd been staring at her. If he couldn't banish the images of her from the past when he was alone, what chance did he have with her in his home?

"Let me take your coat," he said, hanging it on a nearby coat tree to dry. "It's soaked. And so are you," he said, when he turned toward her.

"My umbrella failed," she said, laughing in a clear tone he sometimes heard in his dreams. When she held up the umbrella which had been turned inside out, he laughed, too. "The wind is incredible. And it's not letting up anytime soon."

"Welcome back to Oklahoma." Michael nervously clapped his hands together, not wanting Josie to know how her presence upset him. Their time together at church yesterday had proved to him that his control around her was slipping, and until he could get a better grip on his heart, he wanted to limit the time they spent together.

"I'd forgotten how many storms we get in the spring and early summer."

Michael suddenly became aware that she clutched

her briefcase. "Let me get you a towel. The water will ruin the leather."

"How about one for my hair, too? I can't believe how wet I got running across the driveway."

Michael returned with towels, and then forced himself to turn away as she dried her hair because it seemed inappropriate for him to witness the intimate moment. Taking a deep breath, he busied himself drying the briefcase.

"What brings you out on such a wet day?" he asked. It was the first day since their *engagement* that they hadn't made any plans to see each other. Josie had said she needed to visit Stephanie in the morning and Gran in the evening, as well as run a few errands. He'd been relieved when she hadn't insisted they meet for her parents' sake.

"Change in plans. I need a place to crash for a couple of hours." Her eyes pleaded for his compassion. "If I can borrow a table, an electrical outlet and a telephone jack, I promise you won't know I'm even here," Josie said.

Yeah, right, Michael thought.

"Make yourself at home." What else could he say? *No, you have to leave because you're filling my thoughts day and night.* Or better yet, *Please stay, because the more I'm with you the more I'm convinced you're still the woman of my dreams?*

"Oh, thanks." Josie flung her arms around him and hugged him tightly, but briefly. When she backed away awkwardly, he knew she fought the same ghosts from the past that taunted him. To cover her distress, she rushed on. "I had a great time with Stephanie and the baby, but then Gran didn't feel well enough to visit this afternoon. When Mom learned I was at loose ends, she decided we should work on wedding plans."

Michael nodded with understanding.

"I had to escape. And you're the only excuse she would accept."

"Glad to be helpful," Michael said, trying to inject some humor into the moment.

"I've brought work for a future project the charity is considering. I'll be as quiet as a mouse." Josie patted her briefcase.

A cute mouse, Michael thought, as he cleared the dining room table. "How's this?"

"Perfect."

He started to leave the room.

"Michael...if it wouldn't be too much trouble, could I fix a cup of hot tea?"

"No problem. You settle in. I'll get it for you."

"I could get it myself—"

"It's no problem." In the kitchen, Michael filled a glass measuring cup with water and put it in the microwave to heat. He poured the near-boiling water into a small teapot his mother had left behind and added tea bags to steep.

From the back corner of the kitchen, he had a clear view of Josie. Just the thought of her making herself at home in his kitchen had unnerved him. He didn't want to make new memories with her in his home. In less than a month, she would be gone, and he didn't want her to leave the slightest trace behind. He didn't want to walk into an empty room and smell her perfume or hear her laughter or listen for her voice to call his name.

Careful not to spill the tea, Michael carried the cup and saucer into the dining room.

"Mmm, this smells divine. What flavor is it?" She blew gently across the top of the warm liquid, then took a sip.

"Country Peach Spice." Michael hoped she wouldn't prolong the conversation.

"I'll have to buy some to take back with me." She took another sip, then held the china cup up for inspection. "I love this china cup, too. The rose pattern is so familiar."

Michael briefly closed his eyes. What had he been thinking? "It should. You gave it to my mother for her birthday."

"Of course," Josie said, the slight smile telling him she remembered.

"Mom loved it," Michael quickly explained. "But when they moved to Florida, she had to downsize. Since I was moving into the house, she left behind what she didn't have room to take but couldn't bear to sell or donate." And Michael hadn't been able to get rid of the cup and saucer either.

"You wouldn't believe all the things she left," Michael added, not wanting Josie to think his mother had purposefully left behind items connected to her and Michael. "Well, the furniture is obvious, but she also left me dishes and doilies and porcelain knick-knacks. She said I would be inheriting them one day anyway. And of course, she spread her generosity equally amongst my sisters."

Josie continued to study the pink rose pattern. "I'm touched she kept it all these years."

"Mom loved these cups and saucers. She used them all the time," Michael exaggerated. He clearly recalled the look in his mother's eyes when she'd given them to him. "Go after the girl," she'd said. "Go after her."

He hadn't gone after Josie, but he had kept the teacups.

"Well...I don't want to keep you from your work," Michael said.

"Me, neither."

"I'll be upstairs in my office. Yell if you need anything."

Josie pulled her laptop from the briefcase, set it on the table, then pressed her index finger against her lips. "Quiet as a church mouse," she said.

Michael nodded, then determined not to show his eagerness to leave her, ascended the stairway at a leisurely pace.

Once upstairs, he slouched in his office chair and covered his face with his hands. Any hope of working on future teaching plans had vanished the second Josie entered the house.

The minutes crept by, and she kept her promise. Quiet as a church mouse. Yet, her memory stormed through his mind with a volume he couldn't turn down.

He flashed back to yesterday morning at church. From across the entryway, he'd glanced up just as she'd cradled Stephanie's baby against her chest. His stomach had churned and burned, and his heart had ached at the precious sight. Josie's tenderness had drawn him to her side, and as though he hadn't been able to help himself, he'd had to touch her and the baby at the same time. He'd had to know what it would feel like to have a baby with Josie. For just a second, he'd allowed the old dream to live.

When Josie had handed the infant back to Stephanie, he'd wanted to reach out and say, "Hold her just a little bit longer." And then, still caught up in the moment, he'd kissed Josie on the lips as if they still belonged together.

It'd taken nerves of steel to get through the sermon without showing his torment. Then just when he'd thought he'd regained control, his hands had touched Josie's as they'd held the hymnal. He'd never sat through a longer sermon, despite the fact Pastor Conner finished early.

And now Josie Marshall sat downstairs sipping tea from a rose-patterned cup and saucer he'd saved.

Michael made one more attempt to work on school plans, then abandoned the idea totally. He needed to do something physical that would vent his swirling emotions. But it had to be something upstairs, away from Josie. And something quiet that wouldn't attract her curiosity.

A quick walk through the upstairs rooms reminded him that he needed to clean out his walk-in closet. He'd been saving the tedious project for a rainy day, and this was the day.

In time, he worked his way to the bottom of the built-in cabinet. Eager to be finished with organizing the closet, he opened the bottom drawer, saw the black velvet box and immediately slammed the drawer shut.

Like a tire that had suddenly gone flat, Michael slumped to the carpet. While he hadn't actually forgotten he kept the jeweler's box in this drawer, the cleaning project had temporarily distracted him to the point he'd opened it without thinking about what it held.

Now that he'd opened the drawer, he couldn't ignore the box. Michael waited until his breathing slowed, then cautiously opened the drawer again. He removed the small box, brushing the soft nap against his palm. He swallowed, then respectfully snapped open the lid.

The emerald ring had belonged to his grandmother, Opal. Though Michael had been young when she'd died, he'd loved her dearly and had wonderful memories of time spent at his grandparents' lake home. After living to see their sixty-fifth wedding anniversary, according to family tradition,

Grandmother Opal had bequeathed the ring to Michael at her death with the hope he would someday know the kind of love she'd shared with her husband.

Michael pulled the platinum ring from the box and pushed it as far as the first knuckle on his pinky, then he walked into the bedroom. Beneath the ceiling light, its brilliance reflected across the room.

Instantly, Eddie's challenge filled his mind. *I won't believe you and Josie are engaged until I see a ring on her finger.*

All along, he'd known he would have to give this ring to Josie. He'd put it off as long as he could.

Michael shoved the ring back into the box and then set it on top of the bureau. Sitting on a wooden chair across the room, he studied the ring box.

Within seconds, the old bitterness and anger consumed him. The ugly emotions grasped his heart and twisted it until all he could remember were the bad times between him and Josie. Mentally traveling back in time, he once again heard her say, "I'm taking the job abroad." As the memory played on, he watched her hand the engagement ring back to him and say, "It's best this way." He'd stood there, dumbfounded, thinking it had to be a bad dream, only to realize the nightmare was forever.

Michael slammed his fist against his palm. The plan had seemed so simple and fail-proof. He and Josie would pretend to be engaged. They would hold hands in public, smile at one another at just the right moment and be seen together at church and around the city. Then as soon as the court awarded him permanent custody, Josie would go back to London, and he and Sharla would begin their lives as father and daughter.

But it wasn't simple.

He hadn't counted on the old memories, both the good and the bad, to come out of hiding. Not only did Josie constantly remind him of their painful past, but she illuminated the future he'd lost.

Michael rubbed his eyes, then pushed his fingers through his hair. But beyond his old love for Josie, something else troubled him. He hadn't expected the deceit to wear on his soul.

He'd been so certain God had sent Josie to him to help him gain custody of Sharla that he hadn't truly considered the spiritual ramifications of his plan. Could God honor this fight for Sharla when he had to be dishonest in order to win the court case?

Michael shook his head. He couldn't afford thoughts like this. Sharla had been through too much in the last year, and a loving God wouldn't want her to suffer anymore. Michael had to gain custody of Sharla. And in order to do so, he had to put his grandmother's ring on Josie's finger again. But it galled him to give her this ring, to see it on her finger when it would mean nothing to her.

The clock ticked loudly, counting the minutes. In no hurry, Michael waited until he had calmed and the memories had retreated. He looked out the window, aware the rain had lessened and the sun had dissolved the black clouds.

Descending the stairs quietly, he sneaked up on Josie. Wearing reading glasses, she focused on the laptop screen. Beside her lay a pen and a yellow legal pad with scribbled notes. Pausing, he watched her work. She bit down on her bottom lip as if the information she read fascinated her. Then as if she'd sensed his presence, she laid the pen down and cautiously looked up.

Though she didn't speak, her eyes widened with curiosity.

Michael shoved his hand into his pants pocket and fingered the velvet ring box.

"Can you take a break?" he asked.

"Sounds important," she said, closing the laptop lid.

"It is. There's something we haven't discussed, and I've just assumed you understood it would be part of the charade."

Her eyes widened even farther, this time with trepidation.

Clutching her hands beneath the table, Josie tried to hide her concern. Michael's serious eyes set off alarms in her mind. What could they have forgotten?

"Let's go into the living room," Michael suggested.

Josie grabbed her teacup and followed silently. Pressing both hands around the warm china, she felt a tiny bit of comfort, but not nearly enough to ease her mind.

Glancing back at the laptop and her notes, she noticed her shoes remained by her chair. For such a long afternoon, she had little to show for the hours she'd spent working. But had she really thought she could concentrate with Michael upstairs in the room directly overhead? She'd heard every step, every door he'd opened, and even every frustrated sigh. If the house had been any quieter she would have heard his heartbeat.

When Michael had made it plain he didn't want her making herself at home, she'd found herself instantly drawn to the kitchen. So after she'd finished the first cup of tea, she'd helped herself to a second and third cup, and finally she'd steeped a whole tea-pot of Country Peach Spice. Being in the kitchen calmed her nerves. As her mother's, this kitchen was cozy and welcoming and felt like home to her.

Josie took a sip of tea and nervously pressed the warm cup against the side of her face. Looking out the large window, she noticed a bright cardinal perched on a nearby branch, his brave presence announcing the storm had passed.

"Is there a problem?" Josie asked. Michael had paced the room twice and his growing agitation scared her. "Oh, no," she said. "We've been found out, haven't we? And if they tell the caseworker this could destroy your chances of gaining custody." And all this time they'd spent together and all the old memories she'd had to face would have been for nothing.

"Everything is still on track," Michael assured her.

"Then what is it?" Josie began to lose her patience.

"It's something Eddie said."

Josie shook her head. Eddie had said a lot of things, but nothing that should have ignited this kind of worry.

"He said, 'I won't believe you're engaged until I see a ring on her finger.'"

"Oh," Josie said, lifting her chin high then letting it fall as she stretched the syllable like taffy. "An engagement ring."

Michael held his hands out palms up as if the matter were beyond his control.

"But Michael, an engagement ring is expensive. And I don't think they'll let you take it back when you call off the wedding."

Granted, they needed to do everything possible to make the engagement seem real, but buying a ring seemed ridiculous.

"If you think it's absolutely necessary, we could start looking." Though a jewelry store was the last place she wanted to spend an afternoon with Michael. "I'm sure we could stretch the process out long enough to get us off the hook. I could pick out a ring that had to be special ordered. What do you think?"

Michael shook his head.

When she dared, Josie met his gaze, and his eyes said exactly what she'd feared. There was only one ring her mother would expect Josie to wear, and any other would send up warning flags.

Michael pulled the black velvet box from his pocket and handed it to her. Josie shuffled the box from hand to hand as if it were a hot potato. She didn't have to open it to know it held Grandmother Opal's emerald ring. A ring she'd once worn at a time when she'd promised to love and cherish Michael forever.

Finally, she opened the box and gasped. The ring was far more beautiful than she'd remembered. It radiated everything she'd always wanted in life: hope, love and peace.

Without thinking she took the ring from the box and fingered it. Moving to the window, she held it in the sunlight and watched its brilliance dance around the room and across Michael's solemn face. When temptation and curiosity grew stronger than her will, she slipped the ring on her left index finger. The ring circled her finger as if it belonged there.

Too late, she realized what she'd done.

"It's...I always..." she began, the words stumbling on her tongue. "I always loved this ring. It's so beautiful. The craftsmanship is exquisite." She tried to focus on the ring as if it were a museum object and not a symbol of everlasting love.

Inside Josie crumbled. How could she have been

so ignorant? To put this ring on her finger had been insensitive. Though Michael stared in silence, she felt the chill. Anger sparked in his dark eyes as his mouth and brows twitched.

She wondered if the torment she felt was written on her face for Michael to decipher. Once, this ring had been the symbol of their love, now it was nothing more than a painful reminder of all they'd lost.

Josie closed her eyes and silently prayed for the strength to do the right thing. She couldn't rip the ring off her finger, because that would say the past had meant nothing to her. But she couldn't wear it for the rest of her hiatus, either. That would be akin to driving a stake through her heart.

Taking a deep breath, Josie decided to slowly remove the ring. But when she pushed on the platinum band, it wouldn't budge. Not because her finger had suddenly swollen. But because she couldn't bear to take it off. Giving the ring back the first time had nearly killed her, to do so again would surely destroy her heart.

Oh, God, Josie prayed. She'd been so certain He had brought her home to renew her weary faith, but with each passing day she became more and more convinced that He'd brought her home to deal with Michael and her old memories. The trouble was, she wasn't sure what to do with those old feelings. She wasn't sure what lesson God was trying to teach her. She only knew her heart ached.

Looking at the ring, thoughts of settling down

with a husband and children flashed through her mind. Desperate to rationalize, she blamed the errant images on the turmoil in her life. She was at a crossroads, and in a few weeks she would be faced with a major decision. Marriage was an option, albeit an unlikely option. To get married she would have to fall in love with a man who wanted to spend the rest of his life with her. And one look at Michael's face told her he wished their paths had never crossed this summer.

With the ring still on her finger, Josie said, "I don't have to wear this. We can stall. We can say it needs to be repaired, and because it's an antique it has to be sent off to an out-of-town jeweler who specializes in this type of work."

Michael shook his head. "Your mother knows the ring was in mint condition the day you gave it back. She's not going to buy that story."

"You're right," Josie conceded. "I'll only wear it in public, and I promise you I'll take extra special care of it, because I know some day you'll want to give this to…"

She couldn't finish the sentence. She couldn't imagine another woman wearing *her* ring. And by the anguished look on Michael's face, neither could he.

When he moved toward her, she didn't back away. He took her hand, studied the ring, then raised her fingers to his lips. Her heart beat faster, and a voice in the back of her head warned her to run as fast as she could. But her feet refused to move.

Leaning against him, she closed her eyes as his arms circled her waist. Arching her neck, she anticipated the warmth of his kisses as his lips slid down her skin. For a second, he buried his head in the side of her neck, and she thought he might pull away. Then his embrace tightened. When his lips sought hers, they kissed as if their engagement had never ended.

The kiss rattled Josie with the power of high wind gusts. She felt shaken and drained, believing the tender moment had lasted for hours instead of seconds. Dealing with the old memories would be nothing compared to trying to forget this kiss.

This kiss was the reason God had brought her home.

This kiss was the beginning of their end.

How could he have kissed her? Michael wondered as he pounded a nail, hit his thumb and dropped a shingle. It was late afternoon and the sun had dried the playhouse roof. This was the third time he'd smashed his thumb and it seemed just punishment for his stupidity.

And what angered him even more than the kiss was knowing he'd wanted her. In that moment, he would have forgiven her anything to have one more chance. For her to wear the ring for real.

Michael pounded nail after nail, but he couldn't

vanish the kiss from his thoughts, especially when
he could see her swinging on the wooden swing beneath the old maple tree in her parents' backyard.
Stopping to wipe his brow with a handkerchief, he
glanced toward Josie as she extended her hand to
admire the ring. Kissing her had been a huge mistake. She'd been just as defenseless as he'd been to
the old feelings, and there was no telling what sig-
nals he'd sent her.

He sighed, hating to admit he was still vulnerable
to this spirited woman. But maybe the kiss was his
salvation. It was a reminder that he needed to guard
his heart lest he be tempted again.

No, he wouldn't let Josie break his heart a second
time. God had given her dreams that encompassed
the world, while his remained rooted in Tulsa. In
less than four weeks, she would get on a plane and
leave him.

But if their love wasn't meant to be, why did he
still feel drawn to her? And why hadn't he found
anyone who filled his heart as Josie once had?

Michael pounded nails as fast as he could. With
the last shingle in place, he glanced over at Josie
again, but she was gone and the empty swing glided
through the air. Hearing a loud tapping, he angled
his body toward her bedroom window, being careful
to shift his weight and steady himself.

Josie leaned out her window and blew him a kiss.

"Truce," he said though she couldn't hear him,
then he blew the kiss back.

If he'd known how easily Josie would have wiggled her way into his life, he would never have asked her to help him gain custody of Sharla. But that wasn't true, either. He would do anything to guarantee Sharla's future. He didn't care what the cost was to his heart. Didn't the past prove that his happiness didn't depend on Josie Marshall?

Chapter Ten

Chapter Ten

"**I**s that what I think it is?" Sarah asked, her eyes brighter than the emerald on Josie's finger.

As Josie held out her hand to let her mother admire the ring; she nervously clenched her free hand. All afternoon, she'd dreaded this moment. Only after spending hours on the old backyard swing had she summoned enough courage to show her parents the ring.

"We're so happy for you," her father said, putting his arm around her shoulders and squeezing tightly.

Joyful tears flowed down her mother's face as she completed the family hug.

With her face buried in her parents' loving embrace, Josie begged God to help her find a way through her pretend engagement that would spare her parents' feelings. It was way too late to spare her own heart.

Letting her tears fall, she smiled, convincing her parents she cried with them while inside her heart twisted in regret. Looking back, she could see she'd made the wrong decision. Honorable intentions or not, she had satisfied her own selfish desires and hadn't waited to hear God's voice. She'd charged ahead, believing that by helping Sharla she could make amends for Angelina's death, and now she had to honor the commitment she'd made and pray she could leave Tulsa without hurting her parents. All her life, they had trusted her and loved her unconditionally. If they knew the whole truth, they would be so disappointed in her.

"This calls for a celebration," John said.

"Of course it does. Let's go out to dinner," her mother exclaimed. "And we have to call Michael."

Sarah had the phone in her hand before Josie could say, "He's working on the playhouse tonight. I'm sure he's grubby and tired. We'll celebrate later—tonight I'd rather be with the two of you."

A disapproving light flickered in her mother's eyes, warning Josie she'd said the wrong thing.

"I mean the four of us can celebrate tomorrow night. Gran, too, if she's feeling up to an evening out. Dinner would be wonderful." She tried to correct the mistake, but it was too late. Once her mother grabbed on to an idea, she didn't let go.

"Of course, we'll go to dinner tomorrow night.

But we also have to have an engagement party. Especially if you'll be getting married by the end of the summer. And we've got to get moving on those wedding plans or you might not be able to book your first choice of florist, caterer, photographer...and we'd better talk to Pastor Conner and make sure the church is available. Oh dear, you haven't even set a date!''

Josie looked to her father for help, but he shrugged his shoulders as if to say it would be easier to stop an out-of-control ocean liner than to prevent his wife from planning her daughter's wedding.

Before Sarah could punch in a telephone number, Josie took the receiver from her hand and hung it up. ''We'll get started on the wedding plans tomorrow. I promise. But tonight, I would like to spend the evening with my two favorite people.''

Josie linked arms with her parents and smiled as if she were the happiest girl in the whole U.S.A. Behind her, the second hand ticked noisily on the kitchen clock. It was going to be a long night.

At her father's suggestion, they ordered a large cheese-and-mushroom pizza for delivery. While they waited, they made a garden salad and chilled a bottle of sparkling water. The harmony between her parents amazed Josie. Stepping back, she watched them work. When her mother nodded and pointed, her father knew exactly what she needed. Rubbing shoulders, they chopped carrots and cucumbers and tomatoes, chatting on about the day and wedding plans.

Josie quietly slipped from the room, craving the safety of her bedroom. Curling up in the window seat, she rested her chin on her knees and wrapped her arms around her legs. Her parents had the kind of marriage she wanted, the kind of relationship she'd once believed she'd had with Michael.

Looking toward heaven, she asked God, "How did Michael and I mess things up so badly?"

Biting down on her lip, Josie faced her worst fear. What if Michael was the man God had intended for her to marry? The man she would have shared her parents' kind of love with. But she had messed that relationship up, and there was no going back. Did that mean the man she would marry would be only second-best?

"Forgive me, Father, for my youthful arrogance and immaturity. In the next few weeks, please show me the new path you have chosen for me and help me take the first step in this new direction."

Though Josie didn't hear a clear answer in her heart, for the first time in months, she felt as if God had heard her plea.

When Josie woke up in the middle of the night and couldn't go back to sleep, she took a blanket and crawled into the window seat. Snuggled comfortably amongst her childhood stuffed animals, she gazed at Michael's home and backyard. All the

lights were off in the white clapboard house, indicating he slept peacefully without worry. A bright
lamp perched at the top of the garage shrouded the
playhouse in a soft light. From the outside, the miniature Victorian house looked complete with its cedar roof, stained-glass windows and yellow walls
with white gingerbread trim. Still, Michael would
have to continue working overtime in order to finish
the interior by the time the judge decided Sharla's
custody case.

Josie closed her eyes and said a brief prayer for
Michael and Sharla, hoping God would allow the
judge to see as she had that they belonged together.

As she continued to pray, her mind wandering to
her own troubles, the words from a sermon she'd
heard long ago came to mind.

*When we feel distanced and cut off from God, it
isn't because He's turned His back on us, but because we've turned our backs on Him.*

Josie dared to open her eyes and through a haze
of tears stared at the heavens. As she turned back
toward God, so many things became clear. He hadn't
disowned her. He hadn't stopped listening to her or
answering her prayers. No, she was the one who'd
turned away. She'd been so devastated and angered
by Angelina's death that she'd walked away from
God. She hadn't understood how He could let the
innocent child die in her arms.

Oh, Lord, Josie prayed. *Forgive me for being angry and resentful when I needed You most. Even*

though I only knew Angelina for a short time, she was a huge blessing in my life, and I loved her dearly. I will never forget her. She's the child who made me think about settling down and having my own family. She taught me to appreciate the moment, as well as the small blessings in my life. I may never understand why You took her to heaven, but deep in my heart I believe You were with her always...even now.

Tears streamed down Josie's cheeks as she remembered Angelina's grand smile and the cheery lilt of her voice. Wiping her eyes with the blanket, she knew Angelina wouldn't want her to wallow in sorrow. Neither would she want Josie to remain angry at God. She would want Josie to reach out to God and move on with her life.

Raising one hand in the air, Josie opened her heart to God, and for the first time since losing Angelina she let His love comfort her. Resting her head on her knees, she asked God for the strength to keep her promise to Michael and Sharla.

Angelina's life had changed Josie's forever, and now it was time for her to stop walking in anger and sadness and to cling to the girl's loving legacy.

As Josie's parents expected, Michael joined them most mornings for breakfast. On those mornings, Sarah insisted on fixing Michael's favorite—scrambled eggs and salsa—for everyone. In a very short time, bonds had been reestablished and family traditions begun.

Josie's father kissed her goodbye and shook Michael's hand, then walked with his wife to the front door.

The second they were alone, Michael leaned across the table and said in a low voice, "You look different today."

Josie shrugged her shoulders as she fingered the emerald ring. "I don't know what you could mean. I haven't changed my hairstyle or makeup or bought any new clothes since I've been home."

"No, I'm talking about the warm glow in your eyes. There's definitely something different."

Josie bit down on her lip, then smiled. Everything was different, but she didn't feel like she owed Michael an explanation. "Let's just say I've found a little of that peace I've been searching for."

Michael rubbed a strand of her hair between his fingers, then released it. "You're more beautiful than ever."

"Thank you," Josie said, lowering her head, feeling the instant heat redden her cheeks. They hadn't talked about the kiss, and she knew they never would. She'd blown him a kiss of truce, and he'd accepted. They both had feelings they didn't know what to do with, feelings that were strong enough to incite turmoil, but too weak to build a future on. But no longer would Josie tuck those emotions into the dark corners of her heart. God had brought her home to face them so she could move on with her life.

Raising her head, she looked directly into Michael's dark eyes. "I am different," she said. "For the first time in a long time, I'm in sync with God and seeking His path for my life."

A path that will take me far away from you, she thought.

Michael opened his mouth to speak, but before he could respond, Sarah entered the kitchen. She dropped a calendar on the table, then placed a hand on each of their shoulders. "We've got work to do. And the first thing on the list is picking a wedding date."

Josie and Michael looked at each other and laughed. They had stalled as long as they could, and now that Sarah's patience had worn thin they knew life would be a lot easier if they chose the course of least resistance.

Michael pushed the calendar toward Josie, and she shot him a glance that said *Gee, thanks.*

As Josie flipped the calendar pages past August and into September, Sarah cleared her throat. "You said it would be a summer wedding."

Michael gently rolled back the pages, stopping on August.

Josie quickly pointed to the last Saturday of the month. "This is the perfect date," she exclaimed.

"Oh, honey, I don't think so," Sarah said.

"School starts at the end of the month. We

wouldn't have time for a proper honeymoon," Michael explained with a twinkle in his eyes.

For a second, Josie wondered whose side he was on. Then she reminded herself that he was merely playing the role of an infatuated man.

"Okay, how about the second Saturday?"

"I think the first Saturday of August would be much better."

"Mo-om," Josie said, stretching the tiny syllable as if it were a rubber band. "Why don't you just pick our date?"

"I would be happy to," Sarah said as she flipped the calendar back to June. How about—"

Josie grabbed the calendar from her mother's anxious hands. "Okay. We're getting married the first Saturday in August."

Immediately, Michael grabbed her by the waist and hugged her, then released her to embrace Mrs. Marshall.

Josie glanced at her engagement ring, and for just a second, she wished Michael really did love her.

"Mother!" Josie exclaimed when the church newsletter came in the mail.

"Oh, you've seen the announcement," Sarah said. "I also mailed invitations to our local family and friends who don't attend our church." With both hands in the flower bed, she gave Josie only half her attention. "I thought it would be best if you contacted Michael's family in Florida. I doubt they'll be able to come on such short notice, but I want them to know they're invited. And you'll need to call Sharla and Grandma Rubee, too.''

Josie shook her head. At least her mother hadn't contacted Michael's family or Grandma Rubee. And neither would she. She'd tell her mother they sent them their best wishes, but couldn't make it on such short notice.

''How could you do this without my approval?''

Sarah leaned back on her heels and wiped her brow with the back of her hand. ''Dear, if I had waited on you, there wouldn't be an engagement party on Friday night. As it is, pulling a party off by then is going to be a lot of work. And we were lucky fellowship hall was available on such short notice.''

''Well, what can I do to help?'' Josie asked, knowing when she'd lost the battle.

''Not a thing dear. I've got everything under control.''

That was exactly what Josie feared.

Josie went shopping at the mall on the morning of the engagement party and bought three new dresses, complete with accessories. By six-thirty that evening, she'd tried on the three outfits and hated them all. The short black silk dress was too formal though it did look beautiful with the pearls Gran had given her, the floral chiffon would have been perfect had she been going to a garden party, and the navy evening suit made her look too stunning.

Once again she searched through her closet hoping to find a long forgotten dress that would be perfect for the evening. But no such dress existed. Anything she'd left behind was better suited for a college student. Before she left town, she promised herself she would clean out the closet and donate the clothes to a local charity.

A soft knock at the door reminded Josie time was running short.

"Come in," she called, knowing it was her mother.

"Oh, dear," Sarah said. "I should have come sooner."

Dresses, skirts and dress slacks puddled around Josie's feet, across the floor and over the bed and window seat. The mess amused her, in an odd way, and calmed her nerves. She was making too much of the evening. After all, it really wasn't her engagement party.

Finally, she turned toward her mother. "Oh, Mother, you look absolutely beautiful," Josie said, tears forming in her eyes.

Sarah lifted her hands out to her sides and turned slowly. The pale-yellow linen suit whispered class and elegance, while the sapphire brooch reflected the splendor in her eyes. But Sarah's beauty ran far deeper than linen and high heels, and Josie prayed that one day she would grow into her mother's suit of kindness, compassion and spiritual grace.

Mr. Marshall chimed in from the doorway, "With

the two most beautiful women on my arms, I'll be the envy of every man in the room.'' Then he noticed the pile of clothes. ''My, my. Do we have a problem here?''

''Nothing that five minutes can't fix,'' Sarah said, taking charge and whisking her husband from the room. Quickly, she surveyed the options, then chose the navy evening suit. ''You'll be stunning. The blue makes your eyes dance.''

Josie held the dress to her body, then looked in the mirror. Her mother was right. She looked exactly as she'd always dreamed she would look on the night of her engagement party.

Sarah helped Josie slip into the suit, and then handed her a box.

''What's this?'' Josie asked, surprised by the gift.

''It's something I've been saving for this moment. Gran gave them to me on the night of my engagement party. And now I want you to have them.''

Josie carefully opened the box and removed the pearl-and-diamond stud earrings she'd seen her mother wear a hundred times. ''These are yours to enjoy. They belong on you.''

What Josie wanted to say was that she didn't deserve this gift, because this wasn't the special moment her mother believed it to be. Still, Josie, deeply touched by her mother's love, accepted the gift. She would wear the treasured earrings this night, and like Cinderella, when the clock struck midnight and the engagement was over, she would give them back.

And maybe, if she were lucky, her mother would present them again upon the eve of her real engagement party.

"Let's go," Mr. Marshall called from the bottom of the steps.

"We'll be right there," Sarah said.

As planned by Sarah, Michael waited for the Marshalls at the base of the stone church steps. Josie looked right at him as her father helped her from the car, and when she saw the admiration in Michael's handsome eyes she shivered. She glanced at her mother, touched the pearl earrings, then made a choice she hoped she wouldn't regret. For this evening, she would pretend the engagement was real. She would know once again what it would feel like to be the love of Michael's life. Later, after she'd said goodbye forever, she could look back and savor the memory.

Taking Michael's arm, they followed her parents into the church. With each step, her heart beat faster. Stealing little glances of Michael, his proud carriage overwhelmed her. In the dark suit and starched white shirt, he looked more charming than she'd ever thought possible.

Josie and Michael entered the fellowship hall holding hands. At the doorway, they paused, but didn't dare look at one another. Sarah and her workers had transformed the room into a wedding fantasy. Fresh flowers, white balloons and paper wedding bells filled the spacious room. In the corner, a three-piece string ensemble played quietly while a photographer set up his equipment. But what caught both Michael's and Josie's attention was the collage of photographs which lined the far wall.

The photos drew them both with an unexpected power and magic.

"I don't believe it," Michael said.

"It's unreal," Josie said.

Starting with the summer they'd first met, they followed the trail of smiling faces through memories they'd long forgotten. The glossy pictures told a story of friendship and trust and zest for life and God. They revealed the kind of love that should have lasted forever. Josie stared at the photograph at the end of the memory trail. It'd been taken on the night they'd announced their pretend engagement. Compelled by the smiles and bright eyes, she touched the photo. She'd always heard the camera never lied, but this must have been the exception, because the Josie and Michael in this photograph gazed at each other with the kind of love that took her breath away.

When Michael steered her away from the collage and into the center of the room, Josie followed willingly.

"It is a little overwhelming," Michael said.

"I had no idea a pretend engagement could get so far out of hand."

When the guests started arriving, Sarah led Josie and Michael to the doorway and placed them directly under a white rose- and ivy-covered arch.

There, they greeted old friends and received the many blessings and wishes showered upon them.

At first, Josie felt awkward, but with each shake of the hand and every warm hug, she slipped into the role she'd once believed God had created especially for her. As she relaxed, so did Michael, and she couldn't help but wonder if he, too, was thinking that this was how it should have been between them.

Josie barely had time to glance at Michael as most of the church and half of Tulsa had turned out for the event. The fellowship hall grew hotter and louder with each minute, and Josie longed for a breath of fresh air. Her mouth ached from smiling and her hands had long grown limp from greeting everyone.

Just when she thought she might escape to the ladies' room, she heard her mother call her.

"Josie...Michael...I'd like to get some photographs of the two of you."

The photographer led them to the back of the room near the cake table where he'd arranged potted trees and a stool for a more formal portrait. Much to her mother's dismay, as Josie passed by the cake, Josie stopped to admire it. Fresh daisies and ivy decorated the huge sheet cake that read, Josie and Michael Forever. Feeling suddenly playful, Josie dipped her index finger into the thick frosting on the corner and then licked the gooey confection from her finger. When Michael laughed, Josie dipped another finger into the icing and offered it to him. Holding her palm, he gently licked the frosting from her finger as the camera flashed rapidly.

When their eyes met, Josie lost her breath and felt her legs go weak. She might have fallen had Michael not put his arm around her waist and pulled her close to his chest. With her ear next to his heart, she heard his rapid heartbeat and felt the perspiration on his neck. *Oh, Lord,* she prayed, *if only this magic I feel could last a lifetime.*

From behind, her mother gently pushed Josie and Michael in the direction of the photographer. When Michael dropped his arm and the space between them widened, Josie automatically reached for his hand. Michael caught her fingers and squeezed, pulling her back to his side. Josie marveled at how her body fit against his. She'd forgotten the simple comfort of being close to him, and now that that old craving had been awakened she wanted more. Michael looked down at her and smiled, and in that moment she believed he cared about her more deeply than he'd been willing to admit.

"Josie, I'd like you to sit on the stool. Michael, stand behind her please. Put your left hand on her shoulder and place your right hand..." For ten minutes the photographer called out instructions and clicked the shutter. Despite the lights and the stares of the guests who'd stopped to watch, Josie never lost the feeling that she had a direct line to Michael's heart.

Thinking they were finished, Josie and Michael

moved away from the spotlight. Josie removed the handkerchief from Michael's jacket pocket and wiped the perspiration from his brow.

"One more picture and you're through. I promise," the photographer said.

Josie and Michael looked at each other and rolled their eyes.

"How about a big kiss for the camera?" the photographer suggested in a way Josie and Michael couldn't ignore.

Josie felt the heated blush spread across her face before she dared meet Michael's gaze. The crowd of family and friends blurred into a hazy light and the beat of her heart blasted through the hushed fellowship hall.

In the way she'd always dreamed he would do, Michael hooked his finger under her chin and slowly lifted her face until their gazes met. As he smiled, she felt his chest expand, until his lungs filled with air. It wasn't until she moved toward him that he lowered his mouth to hers and kissed her lightly. Then he hesitated and when she didn't pull away he pressed against her firmly and lovingly. When he started to break away, Josie prolonged the kiss for another second until a boisterous cheer erupted from the crowd.

Josie bowed her head in embarrassment. Before God and witnesses, she'd revealed the hidden secret of her heart. She was falling in love with Michael. And what she felt was more than old love that had been reawakened. She loved the strong man Michael had become and these feelings were far more threatening than lingering memories.

The string ensemble began a new song, and the guests turned back to their conversations. The instant Mrs. Marshall turned her back on the engaged couple, Michael grabbed Josie by the hand and weaving through the thick crowd, led her to a side door where they escaped to a private patio at the back of the church.

Rushing to keep up with him, Josie placed her free hand over her heart and fought to control her excitement. Michael wanted a moment alone. He wanted to finish the kiss they'd started in private. She could hardly believe this was really happening between them.

But as soon as they crossed the threshold, Michael dropped her hand. Moving as far away from her as possible, he removed his jacket and unknotted his tie. Perspiration poured down his face despite the cool summer breeze.

"Wow. I don't know about you, but I needed a break from all the hoopla." Michael's chest heaved as if he couldn't get enough air.

"Yeah, I know what you mean. That's some crowd." Josie chose her words carefully, suddenly uncertain of Michael's intentions.

"Have you ever considered being an actress?" Michael asked, as he wiped his brow with the handkerchief she'd held earlier.

Josie shook her head, feeling her heart deflate.

"You should. That was some performance you gave tonight. Boy, if anyone doesn't believe we're engaged now, they never will."

Afraid to speak, Josie nodded and offered a small smile.

"And I could just hug your mother." Michael paced across the far end of the dimly lit patio as if he were about to burst with energy.

"You could?" Josie backed up until she felt the low, stone wall against her backside.

"Inviting Anne Devon was a stroke of genius. After this, she shouldn't have any doubts."

And neither did Josie. She'd been so wrapped up in the fantasy that she hadn't even noticed the social worker. Truth be told, if she had to list names of who she'd talked to or shook hands with tonight it would be a very short list. She'd had eyes for only one man.

And what a fool she'd been. But at least Michael hadn't seen the truth. He didn't know that what he'd seen and felt tonight wasn't an act. For that she was grateful.

It was over between her and Michael. She needed to get that through her head—and her heart. She needed to quit focusing on him and concentrate on her future—which didn't include Michael and Sharla. She had decisions to make. And if she wasn't careful, her hiatus would be over before she'd determined the new direction God intended for her life.

"I'm glad I didn't know she would be here tonight," Josie confessed. "If I had, I probably would have been nervous and overreacted."

"I'm sure that's why your mother didn't tell us." Michael dusted off a patio chair and sat down. Leaning forward at the waist, he anchored his elbows on his knees and pressed his hands against the sides of his head. Though the only light came through the fellowship hall windows, Josie noticed the tiny lines of worry and fatigue that sparked from Michael's eyes and mouth.

The silence between them made them seem farther apart than just a few yards. In an attempt to bridge the gap, Josie said, "These last few weeks have been much harder than we thought they'd be."

Without looking at her, Michael said, "I never dreamed it would be this complex. I didn't think anyone would make such a big deal about our engagement."

"Never underestimate my mother." When Josie released a small chuckle, Michael glared at her. "Someday, we're going to look back on this summer and have a really good laugh."

"You think so?" Michael asked.

"Yeah," she said, moving to the chair next to his. "Years from now you'll be walking Sharla down the aisle and on that wonderful day all this hoopla will have been worth the trouble. You're going to get custody of her," Josie added.

"I wish I could be as certain as you are." Michael

looked straight ahead as he spoke, clasping his hands tightly as if he couldn't risk the slightest accidental touch.

As silence floated between them again, Josie's thoughts became clearer. There were so many things she wanted to say to him, and even though she wouldn't be leaving town for two more weeks there might not be another intimate moment such as this.

"I haven't lost sight of why we're doing this." When Michael started to speak, she pressed her index finger against his lips to block his words. Then, for just a second, she nearly lost her nerve. "Let's face it, if you hadn't asked me to pretend to be your fiancée we would have ignored each other like we have on all our other visits. But Sharla has given us a gift. We've had this time to reconnect and get to know each other again."

When Michael didn't jump in, Josie nervously continued. "I like the man you've become, and I've learned some important lessons from you this summer. You were right when you said I let life happen to me. I need to quit making decisions based on circumstances. I'm trying to take control of my life, and at the end of my hiatus, after a lot of soul-searching and prayer, I'm going to make some big decisions. Decisions that scare me. But after watching the way you've risked your heart in order to fight for what you believe is best for Sharla, I can see it's the only way to live. I don't want to glide through life and then one day look back with regret."

"Doing what's right usually isn't easy." Michael leaned back in the chair, turning his upper body toward Josie. "As much as I believe I'm the right man to raise Sharla, and as much as I love her, the thought of actually gaining custody terrifies me. Raising a child with a partner is a huge responsibility. Being a single father is even harder."

"Don't let doubt creep in."

"It's hard to fight. Eddie can offer her a ready-made family. That's a huge consideration."

Josie swallowed hard, uncertain if she could push the heavy words off her tongue. "You won't always be alone. Sharla will have a mother and brothers and sisters...soon."

She was glad he couldn't see the tears that gathered in her eyes. Imagining Michael with another woman was too painful to consider.

Michael cleared his throat, choosing to ignore her comment. "I want you to know that you've made a difference in my life as well. Your search to discover God's direction for your life has reminded me that I need to slow down and pray before I charge into situations. I need to recognize when I've convinced myself that my selfish desires are actually God's desire for my life."

She wondered if he was talking about his insistence they pretend to be engaged. He opened his mouth to speak and the look in his intense eyes made her believe he was about to tell her something really important when her mother burst through the door.

"There you are! I've been looking all over for you." Sarah held on to the door until her breathing slowed. "The guests are asking for you. This is your party, after all."

Standing side by side, Josie and Michael smiled and shook hands with family and friends as they left the party. Feeling as if she were in a dream, Josie let her gaze drift around the room taking in the beauty of the flowers, decorations and music one last time.

Stealing a glance at Michael, she was suddenly overwhelmed with how much she had sacrificed for her work. But deep in her heart, she knew that if she could somehow turn back time, she would make the same decision all over again. Working with children abroad was a God-given dream and the path God had chosen for her. She couldn't give up helping the Angelinas in the world.

The path of God was sometimes strange. Because she had loved Angelina so much, she'd been led to help Sharla, and helping Sharla had brought her back into Michael's life. She knew now that God hadn't brought her home to move her into a new career direction. He'd brought her home to experience closure in her relationship with Michael. Until they both completely severed the ties of their hearts, she could never move on with her life and fall in love with someone else. And neither could Michael.

After the last guest left, leaving Josie and Michael alone in the spacious hall, Josie looked at Michael and thought she saw a tear in his eye.

Chapter Eleven

Without a doubt, this had been the saddest night of his life, Michael thought as he walked Josie to the back door of her parents' house and said good-bye as quickly as he could without appearing rude. The instant she slipped inside the house and turned off the porch light, he released a loud sigh.

At home, Michael flung his jacket over the kitchen chair, draped his tie over the stairway banister and dropped his cuff links into a dish on the table in the upstairs hallway. Rolling up his shirtsleeves and pushing his hair from his face, he opened the door to the attic and ascended the narrow steps.

In the attic, he flipped a switch. The harsh light caused him to blink while the smells of cedar and old memories bombarded him. Stacks of cardboard boxes and old trunks covered most of the wooden floor. Rarely used sleds, fishing equipment, and baseball bats from his youth hung on nail pegs on the stud walls. Rushing for the back corner, he ducked his head to keep from hitting the sloping, open-rafter ceiling.

He found the small trunk on the first try. But that didn't surprise him. Not once in the last seven years had he lost track of this box of memories. Blowing dust off the curved top, he picked up the trunk and carried it downstairs to the living room.

After setting the chest on the coffee table, he stood back and looked at it, then circled it a few times. Finally, he slumped in a chair across the room and stared at it for a very long time.

When he summoned his nerve, he slipped a key from his key ring into the lock. Timidly, he opened the lid, ready to slam it shut at any moment.

One by one, he retrieved the letters Josie had written from before their breakup. He had kept them all through the years, starting with the first note she'd scribbled on a napkin in the first grade.

Picking a letter at random, he pulled the fragile paper from the envelope and stared at her neat, loopy handwriting. The bold strokes and soft contours said much more than the words themselves. Josie's cursive held a confidence and a passion for life that still inspired him.

Holding the note close to his heart, he knew the day would come when he would have to get rid of these letters. It wouldn't be right to bring another woman into his home while hiding these memories in the attic. Josie herself had insisted that one day he would marry another woman. But he didn't know if he would ever marry. His feelings for Josie were stronger than he'd imagined possible. And if he'd had any doubts about how he felt, it'd been confirmed tonight.

He'd nearly lost his breath when Josie had stepped from her father's car. Walking into the church with her on his arm had been one of his proudest moments. The instant he'd entered the fellowship hall, he'd known there was nothing pretend about his love for her. Here, in the privacy of his living room, he could admit what he could never say to her. He loved her. He loved her more than he had the day she left him seven years ago. She was the woman he should have married.

Looking in the mirror, he made himself promise he would never tell her. He couldn't risk his heart again. Because just as sure as he told her he loved her, she would still get on the plane and leave him in two weeks.

After spending the morning at the park with Sharla, Michael dropped her off at Grandma Rubee's and then spent the afternoon preparing class plans for the coming year. Though the classroom seemed sedate without the chatter of excited students or brightly colored construction paper projects displayed on the many bulletin boards, he did feel a measure of relief at this neutral territory. Here, in the sanctity of his classroom, he could fight off his worst fears concerning the custody case, and here, his heart was safe from Josie's charming smile.

Not eager to go home to an empty house or the possibility of running into Josie, or—even worse—Mrs. Marshall, Michael decided to stop at a local café for dinner. Even though it was early and a weeknight, Finch's Café did a healthy business and Michael had to wait five minutes for a table. When the hostess showed him to the table by the wall, he thanked her, sat down, and found himself looking directly at Eddie and his new family.

If he could have, Michael would have quietly eased from the crowded café and never acknowledged Eddie Lewis and his family. But before he could, the boy—whom Michael guessed to be about ten or eleven—called out, "Hey, it's Mr. Rawlins."

Michael smiled and waved, recognizing Adam, then walked over to the table.

"Adam, it's good to see you. Are you having a fun summer?"

"The best," Adam said. "We spent the day at Big Splash. Dad's on vacation." Adam beamed with the confidence of a well-loved child.

Eddie quickly rose. "Hello, Michael."

"It's good to see you and your family," Michael said, though he knew the happy image would haunt him for many nights to come.

"I don't think you've met my wife, Amy, or my

stepdaughter, Teresa. But I'm guessing you know my stepson, Adam.''

''I had Adam in my class. He's a great student. How are you Amy?''

''I'm fine,'' Mrs. Lewis said.

Michael extended his hand palm up, offering Adam a high five. Adam playfully slapped his palm, then opened his palm for Michael to reciprocate.

''You've grown a couple of inches since I last saw you,'' Michael said to Adam. To Eddie, he said, ''I taught Adam's third-grade class. I'm sorry I never connected the last names.''

Up to this point, he'd dealt solely with his attorney, the court caseworker, and directly with Eddie. He'd listened to Sharla talk about her stepbrother and stepsister, but had never realized he knew her new family.

''When you taught Adam, I was married to his father.'' Though Michael didn't ask for an explanation, Amy continued. ''After my late husband's death, Eddie adopted my children. That's why we all use the Lewis name. I can understand how that would be confusing.''

''Hey, Mr. Rawlins, would you like to join us?'' Adam asked.

''Thank you for asking,'' Michael said, ''but it looks like you're just about to finish, and I haven't even ordered yet. Maybe another time.''

''That would be great.'' Adam turned his attention

back to the table where the waitress set a huge piece of apple pie in front of him.

Eddie took a few steps away from the table, indicating he would like to talk to Michael in private.

"We haven't said much to the kids." He talked in a low voice.

"I gathered as much. Otherwise, I'm sure I would have heard about it from Sharla."

"We don't want to get their hopes up."

"I've done the same with Sharla," Michael admitted.

"I want what's best for her," Eddie pressed.

"So do I."

"Then how can you fight me on this? Look at my family. I can offer her so much more than you can." Eddie stared at Michael's solitary table.

"Perhaps. But I'm the only father Sharla has ever known. I've been there for her. Let's let the judge decide what's best for Sharla. I'll see you in court." Michael tried to sound cordial but firm.

Eddie nodded, then returned to his family. He obviously told a funny story because Adam and Teresa burst out laughing. However, Eddie and Amy's smiles were tense and pasted on their drawn faces.

Michael tried not to watch the Lewis family, but his gaze kept returning to their corner table. Eddie was right, there were obvious things he could give Sharla that Michael couldn't. But were they more important than what Michael had already given her combined with the love and security he could provide in the future?

The longer he watched the Lewis family, the more anxious he became. He'd almost told Josie at the engagement party about his doubts. Was he doing the right thing in fighting for Sharla by pretending to be engaged or was he merely being selfish?

With his eyes wide-open, Michael prayed God would answer his questions. Not certain he could abide God's response, he paid his check and left Finch's Café. He would fight for Sharla the best way he knew how and leave the decision to the court—and to God.

Josie used every excuse she could to avoid Michael—and her mother. Her brief respite lasted until the following morning, when Sarah told her that Gran had invited them over for tea that afternoon. Josie decided to spend the morning at Swan Lake. With its grassy banks, water irises and lily pads, Josie had always considered it a little piece of heaven. It was a place she had often met God.

As she sipped on her coffee, she pulled a pocket Bible from her purse and began to read from Psalms. The pastoral passages seemed fitting as she watched the swans float across the water with grace and majesty.

She read for a while, then stopped to pray, talking to God with an honesty she'd abandoned at Angelina's death. Time slipped away as she poured out her heart.

A deep peace invaded her soul in this tranquil setting. Opening her eyes, she watched mallards and wood ducks dive for food as the yellow water irises murmured in the summer breeze. While she didn't hear God's voice, she felt Him in her heart. And while this place was special, Josie realized it wasn't because she'd come to the lake that she'd finally found the peace she'd been searching for. She felt connected to God because she had taken time to sit in His presence, to read her Bible, to pray and to listen for His voice in her heart.

In the last six months, not only had she turned away from God, but she'd turned away from all the daily activities that anchored her. And it was those things, such as reading the Bible and praying, that helped keep her on God's track for her life.

Looking up at the cloudless blue sky, Josie prayed, *Dear Lord, thank You for showing me the error of my ways in such a gentle manner. From now on, I promise to make time for You every day. I need You in my life. Without You, I am lost.*

By the time she left Swan Lake, she had a clearer head, a hopeful heart and the courage to face her mother and Gran.

A half hour later as she sat in Gran's living room, she silently debated whether to tell them the truth about her engagement. But every time she had a break in the conversation, the words deserted her.

Finally, she realized confession would only ease her soul while causing pain to the two women she loved most. She'd entered into the fake engagement through her own folly, but she hoped that in the days she had left at home that God would show her a way to resolve this fiasco without hurting the people she loved—though there would be no escaping the pain of her own heart.

Josie smiled as Gran served the tea from a silver tea set that had belonged to her mother. Tears formed in her eyes as she understood how lucky she was to be blessed with such love.

"What is it, dear?" her mother asked, immediately setting her teacup aside and resting her hand on Josie's arm.

"I was just thinking about how much I love being with you and how fast my hiatus is going. Our time together is never long enough."

She waited for her mother to jump at the opportunity to urge her to return home, but neither woman spoke. Still, it was almost as if their silence said more than words could have communicated. Josie looked up and met their wise gazes. They knew. She saw it in their eyes. They knew her engagement was pretend. They knew she'd fallen in love with Michael all over again. They knew she had turned away from God after Angelina's death. Were these things written across her forehead like a newspaper headline?

Inside, Josie panicked. Her hands turned cold and clammy, and her foot began to tap against the floor.

No, she said to herself, calming her nerves. While they might know her heart was in turmoil, they couldn't know why.

"Dear," Gran said in a voice that could quiet a raging sea, "it's only natural to have second thoughts at a time like this. When I married your grandfather, I had jitters right up until we said 'I do.'" Gran paused. Raising a finger, she added, "Come to think of it, I had jitters most of our marriage."

When Gran chuckled, Josie and her mother joined in.

"Your point is well taken, Gran. I'm okay, really, I am," she tried to assure them. As she studied their concerned faces, she realized the main purpose of this tea wasn't to discuss wedding plans, but to let her know they cared and wanted to help her make the sacred transition from single to wedded.

"You're both the best," Josie cried out. Reaching out for the hands of her grandmother and mother, Josie let her tears flow.

Finally, her mother said, "Well, there's nothing like a good cry to cleanse the heart."

"Isn't that the truth," Josie said.

"Now," Sarah said, "about the dress." The conspiratorial look that passed between the two older women alerted Josie.

Their eyes beamed with delight and their faces glowed with anticipation.

"What are you two up to?" Josie asked, feeling suddenly nervous. Pushing her thumb against her emerald engagement ring, she twisted the ring around and around her finger.

"You tell her, Mother," Sarah said.

"No, you tell her, Sarah," Gran urged.

"Well, somebody had better tell me the big secret!"

"It's really no secret," Gran explained. "You know I've kept my wedding dress in storage. Your mother had planned to wear it herself until it'd been necessary for her and your father to wed in a small ceremony. And I...we...would be honored if you would wear my dress. Your mother and I removed it from storage this morning and inspected it. It's in fine condition. And I believe it'll fit you without dieting. You're just the right size."

Josie cocked her head to the left and opened her mouth in astonishment. All her life she'd dreamed of wearing Gran's dress. She'd dreamed of following her grandmother's and mother's steps as women of faith and love. Oh, how she yearned to wear that dress and walk down the aisle to the man of her dreams.

"Yes," she said quickly. "I'll wear your dress." But to herself she said, When I find the man God desires me to marry, I'll wear the dress.

Pausing to find the right words, Josie said, "And

I pray that I'll have the kind of marriage you've both had."

"Now don't idealize your father and me," Sarah warned. "We have our problems just like everyone else. But communication and lots of prayer are the key."

"If you can talk and pray with the man you love, then you can get through any difficult time," Gran added.

"Thanks," Josie said, filing the wisdom away for the future. In God's timing, she would fall in love, get married and have the family she dreamed of.

Chapter Twelve

As soon as Josie walked into the kitchen the next morning and saw the mischievous sparkle in her mother's eyes she knew Sarah was keeping a secret. But before she could quiz her mother, Michael knocked on the back door and Sarah invited him in.

Josie groaned inwardly. Since she'd planned to spend the morning planting begonias and impatiens in the flower beds flanking the front door of Gran's apartment, she'd dressed for garden work. Wearing old blue jeans and a T-shirt she'd found in the back of her closet, her wet hair pulled back in an unflattering fashion, and without makeup, she felt shabby. While any relationship between her and Michael was a dream of the past, she still wanted to look good when she was around him. Years from now she didn't want him to remember her as a frumpy gardener.

"Good morning, Josie," Michael said, kissing her quickly on the forehead. "Garden work? I hope," he teased.

Josie smiled and nodded, wishing she could run upstairs and change. But that would send the wrong signal.

"Gran has given me complete creative control. And I can't wait. In my line of work, I don't get to dig in too many flower beds."

Sarah carried a dish of scrambled eggs to the table while Josie poured the orange juice. Michael, no longer considered a guest at the Marshall's home, found the preserves and salsa in the refrigerator and set them on the table.

Mr. Marshall's spicy cologne alerted Josie to her father's presence before she saw him in the doorway. "It looks like I'm just in time."

"As soon as you say grace, we can eat."

Standing in a circle, Josie reached for her father's and her mother's hands. At the last instant, Mr. Marshall stepped to his wife's side, forcing Josie to take Michael's hand.

"Dear Father," Mr. Marshall began. "Please bless this wonderful food we are about to eat. May it nourish our bodies, as Your love and mercy nourishes our hearts and souls. We thank You for this special time together as Mother and I share in the planning and preparation for Josie and Michael's wedding."

The slight pressure of Michael's hand caused

Josie to lose track of her father's words. His voice grew dimmer as all she could focus on was the steadiness of Michael's grip. The longer the prayer lasted, the colder and clammier Josie's palms became. When she felt Michael nudge the emerald ring with his thumb, she opened her eyes and looked at him. He stared at their entwined fingers with a look of sadness and regret that would have broken her heart if it hadn't recently been shattered.

"May Your peace, oh Lord, fill our hearts. Amen."

"Let's eat before the eggs get cold." Sarah removed a pan of biscuits from the oven and set them on the table. Conversation faded as the food was served.

Josie felt guilty when she looked at the bacon and eggs heaped on her plate. In a third-world country this portion would have fed an entire family. But she wasn't in a third-world country; she was at her mother's kitchen table, and as long as she had food in her mouth, she couldn't talk. And if she couldn't talk, she wouldn't have to answer the questions her mother was certain to ask about the wedding. It wouldn't hurt Michael to be the target of her mother's enthusiasm for a change.

Three bites into the meal, Josie abandoned her silly plan. First, sitting close to Michael, their hands brushing as they reached for salsa and jam and napkins, had caused her appetite to flee. And secondly, the sparkle in her mother's eyes grew increasingly bright with each second that passed.

Putting her fork down, Josie asked, "Mother, what are you up to?"

"Well, now that you ask, there is something you have to see." She promptly retrieved two newspapers that had been hidden in the dish towel drawer and handed one to Josie and one to Michael.

"It's today's *Tulsa World*. And Michael, I'm sorry if you spent time searching for your paper this morning. I picked it up early because I wanted you and Josie to see this together."

"See what?" Josie asked impatiently. Whatever it was, it couldn't be good. "Oh Mother, I hope you didn't go ahead with any kind of announcement."

"Well, if you would open the newspaper you would know."

Michael located the article first. "It's on page two of the Living section."

Josie dropped her paper, and Michael opened his fully to allow her an unobstructed view.

"Oh, my," Josie said as she stared at the photograph of herself and Michael that had been taken at the engagement party. The dreamy haze in her eyes left no doubt she was a woman in love. And now, everyone in Tulsa would know she deeply loved Michael. Josie covered her eyes with her hands and prayed she could disappear.

Michael jabbed her side with his elbow to remind her she'd slipped from the fiancée role.

"Isn't it great?" Sarah asked.

"It's a wonderful surprise," Michael said. "I can't believe you convinced them to run an article and a photograph."

Josie quickly skimmed the short paragraphs anticipating more humiliation, but was pleasantly surprised by the brief description of her and Michael's careers and their recent courtship. The only item she could possibly object to was the assumption that the happy couple planned to live in Tulsa.

"Well, it pays to have connections," Sarah explained. "The editor of the Living section just happens to be the niece of a dear friend. Normally, you're only allowed a small picture and an announcement in the Sunday paper. But when I explained how you both had grown up in Tulsa and had been childhood sweethearts who'd followed their dreams to work with children around the world, she thought it would make a nice human interest piece. And Josie, she'll be calling you later. She'd love to do an article on your experiences abroad."

"That would be great," Josie agreed. At least something good would come out of her public embarrassment. "But Mom, you have to promise me one thing."

"Anything, dear," Sarah said.

"Promise me you won't make any more wedding plans or decisions without my okay or Michael's."

"You've got my word."

Normally, Sarah Marshall was as trustworthy and

honest as they came. But when it came to planning Josie's wedding, Josie didn't trust her one bit.

It was at least an hour later before Michael and Josie had a chance to talk privately.

"Mom, if I don't leave for Gran's *now,* I'll be planting flowers during the hottest part of the day." Josie rinsed her coffee cup and left it in the sink.

"But I'd hoped we'd make more progress this morning with the wedding plans."

Josie and Michael each sighed as they closed a book of invitation samples that Sarah had borrowed from a local printer. When they'd ignored her suggestion to stop by the printer, Sarah had taken matters into her own hands and had the samples delivered to them.

"We need to think about what we've seen." Josie tried to stall. But as the pretend wedding date approached, it became increasingly difficult to come up with reasonable excuses and delays that Sarah would accept.

"Okay, you can think about it today, but if you don't select an invitation by tomorrow morning, I'll pick one for you and order it. As it is, by the time we order them, address them, and mail them, the schedule is going to be tight. Let's just pray nothing goes wrong."

"Yeah," Josie said. "Let's pray nothing goes wrong."

Michael pinched her side, and Josie jumped.

"Careful," he whispered, "your true colors are showing."

"Really?" she teased, as soon as her mother left the kitchen. "I'll show you my true colors." She began tickling him on the stomach, remembering exactly where his most sensitive spots were. Michael laughed so hard tears ran down his face as he begged her to stop.

"I'll make you a deal," Josie offered, hoping to trick him into helping her plant Gran's flowers.

"No deals," Michael said as he gasped for breaths.

"Then I don't stop." Josie began a new tickle attack. Thankfully, she wasn't ticklish or Michael would have been able to strike back.

"Okay. Deal. Truce," he said, blowing her a kiss.

The kiss surprised Josie and threw her off balance. In the split second her weight shifted, Michael grabbed her at the waist, pinning her arms to her sides.

"I've got you now," he whispered.

"So what are you going to do with me?" she asked.

"I wish I knew," he said, his laughter fading into a serious tone. He dropped his arms and backed away as if she were too hot to touch. "I wish I knew."

Josie pushed her hands through her hair and exhaled loudly. "Just another week," she said. "We can make it seven more days."

"I have the feeling it's going to be one long week."

"Michael!" Josie exclaimed. "Is being engaged to me that horrible?"

Michael threw his hands up in the air as if to surrender. "Of course not. You're a breeze. It's your mother that's tough."

"Not so loud," Josie said. "She'll hear you."

Michael walked to the kitchen doorway and peeked down the hallway. "She's nowhere in sight. Boy, if I'd had any idea how tough she would make things, I would never…"

"Don't even say it," Josie said, pressing a finger to his lips. "This is a small price to pay to guarantee Sharla's future."

"You're right."

"However, there is something we need to settle." Josie grabbed her sunglasses and mother's key to the car, then said, "Walk me to the car." She didn't want to take any chances Sarah would overhear the rest of their conversation.

"Mother, we're leaving," Josie called out. When there was no answer, she walked to the base of the stairway and called out a second time. Again, there was no answer. "That's odd," Josie said.

"I wonder what she's up to now," Michael said.

"I have a feeling we don't even want to know."

Josie quickly scribbled a note and tacked it to the refrigerator door. As she locked the back door, she couldn't shake the feeling that whatever her mother was planning, it would change Josie's life forever.

At the car, Michael helped Josie load bags of potting soil and mulch, garden tools and bright multi-colored flats of begonias and impatiens.

"We've got a money problem," Josie said.

Michael rolled his eyes and smiled. "We're not even married yet, and you're already asking for money."

Josie laughed to humor him, while her mind replayed the casual way he'd said *yet*. We're not even married *yet*. Biting down on her bottom lip, she pushed the word *yet* from her mind. There was no *yet* in their case. There was no engagement, and there would be no marriage.

"Seriously, Mother is determined to go ahead with wedding plans. When she places the invitation order tomorrow morning, she'll have to place a down payment. And I suspect she's already placed a down payment on our honeymoon, and who knows what else."

Michael straightened his back and raised his chin proudly. "This is my responsibility, and I'll reimburse your parents for whatever money they lose."

"Thank you. If you'd let me, I would like to pay for half."

"That's not necessary. You're doing this for me and Sharla."

Josie looked down at the lush grass, before meeting Michael's gaze. "Don't kid yourself. I did this for myself. I'm getting as much benefit from this fake engagement as you are."

Placing his hand on Josie's upper arm, Michael asked, "Are you ever going to tell me what brought you home?"

"Sharla brought me home." She knew it wasn't the answer he wanted, but it was the truth. God had brought her back to Tulsa because Josie had needed to help Sharla as much as Sharla had needed her help.

By bedtime, Josie's muscles ached from working in Gran's flower beds. She forced her arms and legs into a few simple stretches, then crawled into bed. Across the driveway, the light in Michael's bedroom came on, and he paced by the window. When he paced by a second and third time, she moved to the window seat for a closer view. That's when she noticed the newspaper in his hand. He'd rolled it up like a log and every time he passed by the window he hit it against his palm. Josie jumped with each whack, feeling his frustration echo through her heart.

Moving to her desk, Josie picked up her copy of the *Tulsa World*. Thanks to her mother's thoughtfulness, this newspaper topped a stack of extra copies of today's edition. With a slightly unsteady hand she opened on the first try to the engagement announcement. Gazing at their photograph she couldn't help but ask herself, *What if?* What if they really were engaged?

With her index finger, she traced the outline of Michael's handsome profile. He was everything she'd always wanted in a man, and yet their love hadn't been strong enough to withstand the pressures of life.

Dear Lord, she prayed, *I can only assume You have a better plan for Michael and me. Help me to let go of him, to sever the ties completely, so we can both move on.*

Using scissors she found in the top desk drawer, she cut out the photograph and pressed it between the pages of her Bible. "Goodbye, Michael," she whispered.

Taking a deep breath, she picked up the telephone and did what she could no longer put off.

Michael answered on the second ring. Because he stood in front of his window, she turned on her light so he could see her as they talked. When she pressed her hand against the glass, he did the same. In that moment, she felt a connection so powerful it scared her. Still, she swallowed, determined not to abandon her convictions.

"There's something you need to know," she said. "I've made a decision."

"You're going back to your work abroad," he said, without surprise.

"Yes. As soon as the hearing is over, I'm leaving Tulsa. I think it's best this way."

"I think it's for the best, too," Michael agreed.

"I hope you find the happiness you deserve, as well as the peace you're searching for."

"I will," she said without hesitation. Thanks to Michael, she'd already found what she'd been searching for. God hadn't abandoned her during troubled times. She'd been the one to turn her back and walk away. God had always been with her, willing to answer her questions and doubts and comfort her sorrowed heart. Even now she felt His presence in this difficult moment.

"Goodbye," Josie said, feeling a finality that made her heart heavy.

"Goodbye," Michael whispered.

For what seemed like a long time, Josie stayed on the line listening to the silence, not wanting to be the first to hang up. Finally, she replaced the telephone receiver. When she did, Michael blew her a kiss. This time, instead of blowing it back, she trapped it with her hand over her heart.

Turning off the light, she slipped to the floor and sobbed. She'd done the right thing, hadn't she? But if so, why did she feel so miserable? Why did she feel like she'd just lost part of her soul?

Michael had known all along she would leave. What he hadn't known was how much it would hurt. Turning out the light, he covered his face with his hands. When she'd first left, he'd been so certain she would come home to him. And she had, though it'd taken seven years. But this time when she left, she wouldn't be back. He'd lost her—and his dreams—forever.

Pulling a blanket and a pillow from the bed, Michael fled the room. He couldn't sleep in this room, in this house, tonight. With her window facing his, and her old letters scattered across his desk, her presence invaded his home.

Locking the back door behind him, he crossed the lawn and entered the playhouse with hopes of forgetting about the past and concentrating on his future with Sharla. He didn't *need* Josie Marshall in his life. He'd proved that during the last seven years. But the trouble was, he *wanted* her in his life. However, once again, she hadn't included him in her dreams.

Michael spread the blanket out on the floor and lay down. In an attempt to put Josie out of his mind, he focused on the playhouse. Only a few finishing details remained. The interior walls needed one more coat of paint, as well as shelves for all of Sharla's books. Once the miniature home was finished, they would shop for a toy box, two chairs and a small table.

While he couldn't wait to see Sharla sitting in the playhouse at the table reading a book or playing tea party with a friend, he also dreaded their day in court. What if he wasn't granted custody? How could he bear to lose both Sharla and Josie on the same day?

Without even trying, his thoughts had come full

circle. Michael tightly squeezed his eyes shut in an attempt to push Josie's image from his mind, but he failed. He would forever remember her standing at the window with her hand pressed against the glass. For just a second, he'd felt as if electricity had passed between them. He'd been convinced she loved him as much as he loved her. But then she'd said the words he'd been expecting. She was leaving him, and this time it was forever.

Chapter Thirteen

Though Josie doubted Michael would make an appearance at breakfast, just to be safe she left the house before her parents awakened. Borrowing her mother's car, she drove to Swan Lake where she contemplated her future during the quiet early-morning hours while watching two majestic swans float across the water.

She'd made her decision. She'd cut her ties to Michael. And she felt a sense of relief that confirmed she'd made the right choice. Her work and the life she'd built were abroad, and she longed to return to the children who needed her love and compassion.

Yet she dreaded leaving Tulsa, because she knew how much her heart would ache as soon as her airplane taxied down the runway. She knew because she remembered every moment of that day seven years ago when she'd boarded the flight that had changed her life in ways she'd been unprepared for. Back then, she'd believed Michael would follow her. That he might even work abroad with her. But those had been foolish wishes. She knew better now. This time, when she boarded the flight to London, there would be nothing to hope for. Not only was her pretend engagement with Michael over, but their friendship as well. She loved him too much to keep pretending they could be friends.

As if the mother swan felt Josie's anguish, she raised her slender head and gazed at Josie for a moment before hurrying to catch up with her mate. Together, the swans glided across the shimmering water, their graceful movements echoing the other's. Josie envied their peaceful harmony. This was the way it should have been between her and Michael.

She waited until her father would have left for work and her mother would have finished washing breakfast dishes before driving home. When she entered the silent house, she called out her mother's name, but there was no answer.

Grateful to be alone, she headed for her bedroom, though she never made it past the living room. The instant she saw the oversize garment bag she knew what it protected.

Gingerly, she fingered the opaque vinyl material and the metal pull tab. She recalled the first time Gran had shown her this dress. She'd been twelve or thirteen, and they'd been looking at family albums on a rainy spring afternoon. Convinced the elegant organza dress with beaded pearls and delicate lace was the most beautiful dress she'd ever seen, she'd declared then and there that like her grandmother, she too would walk down the aisle in this dress. And when she did, she would be headed toward the kind of marriage her parents and grandparents had enjoyed. But now, she knew it took more than a dress—even more than love—for a relationship to survive through the years.

"Mother," she called out. "Mother, are you home?"

She waited for Sarah to come rushing into the room, and when she didn't, Josie felt a huge sense of relief. She wanted to open the garment bag and pull the dress from its hiding place, but only in private. She couldn't risk anyone seeing her hold the dress, because if they did, they would know how desperately she still dreamed of wearing it.

Gently, she pulled the wedding dress from the garment bag. The fabric felt soft and slippery against her skin as she held it against her body. Even without trying it on, she knew it would fit.

Holding the bodice against her chest with one hand, she grabbed the full skirt with her free hand and glided across the room with the grace of a swan. When she turned on her toes, she came face-to-face with her reflection in the large cheval mirror that occupied the sunny corner of the living room.

Josie stopped to stare, and when she did she

couldn't deny she looked into the eyes of a woman deeply in love.

She blamed the weak moment on the dress. She should never have removed it from the garment bag. This time, when she stuffed her love for Michael into the tiny box in the farthest part of her mind, she would never open the box again.

Though she knew she should return the dress to storage, she couldn't resist one last look in the mirror.

The back door banged shut, and Josie froze as Sarah breezed into the living room. Josie's grip tightened on the dress, as if she were a child who'd been caught with her hand in the cookie jar.

"Ooh," her mother sighed with contentment. "I can't wait to see you in this dress. I've been dreaming of this day from the moment I knew I carried you in my womb." Sarah's hands instinctively covered her abdomen.

"Well, don't just stand there. Try it on."

Josie looked at her reflection, knowing she couldn't disappoint her mother. Yet, to try it on this morning would be so painful.

"Okay, I'll try it on," she finally agreed. "But only if you'll try it on first."

Sarah pressed her hand to her chest and backed away from Josie and the dress. "Oh, no, I couldn't," she insisted.

"Please, try it on," Josie pleaded. "It seems wrong to skip a generation. If I'm to walk down the aisle in this dress, I want to know that both you and Gran wore it before me.''

Sarah's eyes filled with a dreamy haze as she took the dress from Josie's hands. When she turned her back, Josie unzipped her mother's dress and then helped her slip into the wedding gown.

''Oh, Mother,'' Josie exclaimed. ''It's beautiful.''

As Sarah gazed into the mirror, old memories clouded her eyes. ''I was heartbroken when your father asked me to change our wedding plans. I had dreamed of wearing this dress, and I was so disappointed when we decided on a smaller wedding in my parents' backyard. But I learned a really important lesson on my wedding day. It's not the wedding that counts, it's the marriage.'' Moving closer to Josie, Sarah caressed the side of her daughter's face with one hand. ''While I hope you have a wonderful wedding, my prayer is that you and Michael will have the marriage of your dreams.''

''I hope so, too,'' Josie said. What else could she say?

Josie stepped back and let her mother enjoy the dress for a few more minutes.

''You know, while I love this dress, I don't think it's me. The suit I wore is more my style. I don't have any regrets about changing my wedding plans. Your father and I had a perfect wedding.''

Josie grinned. Because she'd heard her mother say this more times than she could count, she finished the thought, "It was a perfect day, and you married the perfect man."

"And your day will be just as perfect."

"I hope so."

Josie helped her mother remove the wedding gown and slip back into her own dress. Then she slipped into the wedding dress herself.

The lace bodice accentuated her long neck and graceful shoulders, while the pearled cuffs framed her wrists and emphasized the brilliance of her emerald ring. Josie fingered the platinum band knowing the day fast approached when she would have to take the engagement ring off. While the ring and gown might be perfect fits, she and Michael weren't the perfect match.

"You're more beautiful than I imagined. Oh, Josie, I'm so happy for you." Sarah covered her mouth with both hands.

"Mom," Josie said, "if you're crying now, how are you ever going to make it through the wedding?"

"You know what they say, the harder a mother cries the more happiness the couple shares."

"Who says that?" Josie challenged.

"Okay...I just made it up. But I know without a doubt that you and Michael are going to be happy. I've known since you were children that God has blessed you with a special love and bond that will bring you extraordinary joy through the years."

Josie grew desperate to get out of the wedding

gown, because with every second it grew heavier and heavier with guilt. But before she could change, she heard a knock on the back door followed by a loud bang. Only Michael would knock, but enter before greeted.

"Oh, no," Josie said. "He can't see me wearing Gran's dress."

Sarah gathered up the long skirt and helped her daughter across the living room. At the doorway, Josie paused for one last glimpse in the cheval mirror. She couldn't help herself.

"Too late," Michael said from the opposite side of the room.

Josie looked at her mother and shrugged her shoulders, but Sarah refused to let go of the organza skirt.

"But it's bad luck for the groom to see the bride in the dress before the wedding," Sarah argued.

"It's okay," Josie said. *Because I'm not going to be a bride anytime soon.*

"If you insist." Still reluctant to let go of the gown, Sarah let the pliant fabric slowly slip through her fingers. "I'll be upstairs if you need me."

Michael waited until Sarah left the room before moving closer to Josie. It took all his resolve to keep a safe distance between them.

"You're stunning," he said.

"Thank you." Josie looked down at her clasped hands, as if she didn't dare look at him. Then as if to protect her heart, she shifted her hands to cover the ring.

"I mean you're more beautiful than words could ever describe." Michael felt his resolve gradually desert him, like sand falling through an hourglass. If he didn't leave now, he might...

Swallowing hard, he shoved his hands into his pockets to keep from touching her cheek. The room suddenly became unbearably hot, and perspiration dampened the back of his neck. He had come to talk to her about the upcoming hearing, but that could wait. They still had a few days left to prepare.

"I just remembered something I forgot to do," he said as he hurried for the doorway.

"Michael," Josie said in a voice so tentative, so low, he almost didn't hear her. He stopped, but didn't turn, feeling as if his heart might jump out of his chest.

"Michael," she said again. This time he couldn't resist, and when he turned around he saw more love in her eyes than he believed existed in the world.

"Oh, Josie," he said, crossing the room in three steps. Taking her into his arms, he crushed her against his chest and marveled at how right she felt in his arms. He had no doubt God had made this woman for him.

When her hands brushed the back of his neck, he thought his legs would fail him. Looking into her eyes, he said, "I love you."

"I love you, too."

Lowering his head, Michael kissed Josie with the passion of a man who'd made a lifelong commitment. And when she responded with the same love and adoration he felt, he lost his breath.

The kiss lingered on his lips as Josie pulled away. When he saw the confused look in her eyes, he panicked, and then God's peace descended and he knew exactly what to say.

"This changes everything," he said.

"Does it?" She bit down on her bottom lip, while she twisted the emerald ring on her finger.

"As long as we love each other, we can work out the details." They had to. After this kiss, Josie wouldn't leave him. Or would she?

"You're right," Josie said, standing straighter as if a huge burden had been lifted from her shoulders.

When she smiled, Michael's doubts disappeared. Taking Josie's hand he led her to the sofa and then helped her arrange the skirt of the gown before she sat.

"There's something I'd like to ask you."

Josie nodded as a flash of panic constricted her chest. What if he asked her to stay in Tulsa? What would she say? She'd been so caught up in the moment, so thrilled to know that he loved her as much as she loved him, that she hadn't thought about their future. Swiftly, she prayed for wisdom. Her future hinged on this moment.

"Why did you really come home this summer?" Michael asked.

Josie looked away so he wouldn't see the relief in her eyes. When she felt in control, she said, "I don't know if I can explain why."

"Maybe it's none of my business," he continued, "but I just love you so much, I want to understand what you're feeling. I want to know everything—the good and the bad—that's happened in your life during the time we've been apart. I want to know everything there is to know about you."

Sharing his sense of urgency, she squeezed his hand. "We have a lot of catching up to do."

"The other day you said you came home for Sharla. What did you mean?"

Images of Angelina skipped though Josie's mind. For a long time a wave of pain had accompanied the memories, but in the last few weeks her heart had begun to heal, and now those same images brought comfort as Josie could begin to see a larger picture.

"I came home because someone I loved had died in my arms."

When Michael turned away, Josie realized he thought she'd lost a man she loved. Gently, she placed her hand on his chin, and guided him back to her. "Her name was Angelina, and she was a very special child. She wasn't much older than Sharla. And for a long time I believed I had failed her. If only I could have gotten her to the hospital sooner..."

Wanting to comfort her, Michael put his arms around Josie's shoulders. "I knew when you agreed to the engagement that you understood how deeply I loved Sharla.''

"I had planned to adopt Angelina. I'd just filed the papers. Her entire family had been killed in a village raid. She had no one. When our organization found her, her injuries were so severe they didn't think she would live. As soon as she was stable, I took her back to London and cared for her. She lived with me for two months. But she never recovered..."

Michael embraced her, chasing away her fears and sorrow. Though he didn't say he understood, the comfort and solace she felt in his arms expressed his compassion. As if he had been with her at the time, he finished her story. "And you felt so alone when Angelina died. You felt as if God had abandoned you. And in anger you wondered how God could let the child you loved die."

Amazed he could read her heart so clearly, Josie pulled away, needing to see his eyes. "How do you know?"

"I know because that's how I'll feel if I lose custody of Sharla."

"You won't lose her," Josie promised.

"But you didn't think you would lose Angelina."

"No," Josie said thoughtfully. "And I still don't understand why she had to die. But, I finally realized that I couldn't let her die in vain. I needed to find something good, something precious, in her death.

And that's why I said I would help you fight for Sharla.''

"And if you were to carry it a step further, you could even say Angelina led you back to me."

Josie nodded. "She would have loved you."

"I wish I could have met her. I'd like to thank her for bringing you home to me."

Michael grasped Josie's hands between his, and said, "Thank you for telling me about Angelina."

"I haven't even told Gran or Mother about her."

"That's what makes it so special."

Leaning forward Michael kissed her again, and this time she knew she would stay in Tulsa. But before she could tell Michael, she heard her mother clear her throat.

"You have a visitor," Sarah announced. Beside her stood the caseworker.

When Josie met her mother's gaze and saw the conspiratorial sparkle in her eyes she knew Anne's presence wasn't by accident.

Michael stood, then realizing Josie needed help, extended his hand. Together they walked toward Anne.

Suddenly self-conscious, Josie said, "I was trying on my wedding gown when Michael barged in."

"It's my lucky day whenever I see Josie." Putting his arms around her shoulder he kissed her lightly on the lips. When he exhaled, Josie felt his nerves jolt through her body. "I'm sure you're here for a reason."

"The hearing has been moved to the day after tomorrow at nine o'clock."

"We'll be there," Michael said, pulling Josie into his arms and tightening his hold on her as if she were his life preserver.

Chapter Fourteen

"We can't stand here forever," Michael finally said. Guiding her chin with his fingers, he brought her lips to his and kissed her with the promise of a lifelong love.

"I'm not going anywhere," Josie said, enjoying their newfound intimacy.

"But it might be more practical if you did change clothes."

Josie left a trail of kisses down his cheek and neck as she backed away. "I wouldn't want anything to happen to Gran's dress."

Once more she stood before the cheval glass. No longer did she have to imagine herself as a bride, because in a few weeks she would marry Michael Rawlins.

Mrs. Michael Rawlins. Mrs. Josie Rawlins. The

name fit her as perfectly as Gran's beautiful wedding gown.

"If you'll excuse me, I'll change. Don't go anywhere." Josie made him promise.

"I'll be right here waiting for you. Just like I always have been."

Michael's face blushed at the slip, and Josie rushed back into the living room and flung her arms around him. He had always been here, and in the back of her mind she had believed he was waiting for her. And she wondered if he had always believed she would one day come home to him.

When the telephone rang, Mrs. Marshall answered in the kitchen. "Josie," she called out. "It's for you. Mr. Barrymore."

Josie picked up the living room extension and said hello to her boss. She listened quietly to his news, nodding her head solemnly as he filled in the details. A day ago the information would have devastated her, but today she received it as confirmation that God had sent her home to Tulsa to marry Michael.

Michael knew the second Josie's face grew serious that this telephone call would change their lives. It was one thing to admit they loved each other; it was another to give up a career and move halfway around the world. And he didn't feel it was unfair for him to want her to come home to Tulsa. He'd always known that he wanted to teach, to raise a family, to put down roots in a community. But for Josie it had been different.

Josie had needed to leave home and prove she could make it on her own. It was as if some of her grandmother's wanderlust had been passed down to Josie, because just as Gran had traveled abroad to work with charitable organizations before she'd settled down and married, Josie, too, felt driven to make a difference in the world. But Michael still sensed that Josie felt a deep unrest that compelled her to somehow earn her faith. During the last few weeks, he had witnessed her spiritual growth. She was becoming a woman of unshakable faith, just as her mother and grandmother were.

But he also knew she had some big decisions ahead of her. He and Sharla were a package deal. He had to consider the child's needs. On a whim, he couldn't take Sharla out of school and away from her grandmother to follow Josie around the world.

It all came down to Josie's choice, and for once there were no circumstances to guide her. She would have to choose between him and her work abroad. Anxious to know her decision, he paced around the room as she talked to her boss. If she told him right now that she loved him and wanted to build a life with him in Tulsa, he would be the happiest man in the world.

It seemed like hours had passed by the time Josie finally hung up the telephone. When she looked at him and smiled he knew his worries had been for nothing.

"I'll be staying in Tulsa," she said.

Michael shook his head. "Can you say that one more time? I'm not certain I heard you correctly."

Josie surrounded her mouth with her hands to form a megaphone and then shouted, "I'm staying in Tulsa. I'm staying here with you."

Michael picked her up by the waist and twirled her around the room until they were both dizzy. When her feet hit the floor, but before she could get her breath, he said, "Josie Marshall, would you marry me?"

"Yes! Yes! Yes!"

For the first time since she'd left seven years ago, Michael felt like his world was complete.

Looking up at him, she said, "This is the most incredible day of my life. And after Mr. Barrymore's call, there's no doubt I'm supposed to be with you."

Michael suddenly felt uneasy. "What did Mr. Barrymore say?"

"Actually it wasn't good news for the charity I work for. I've known for sometime that there were financial problems. I'd thought they'd worked them out, but apparently the charity is going to close. It will be a terrible loss, but I trust God will find another means to help the families that depend on our services."

Josie felt Michael pull away before he stepped back. One look at his intense eyes and she knew something was amiss.

"Oh, Josie," he said as if she'd disappointed him in the worst possible way.

"What?" she asked.

"You've lost your job?" he said as if it were a clue.

"Yes. That's why Mr. Barrymore called me. He hated to tell me over the telephone, but he wanted to tell me himself before I heard the news elsewhere."

"Don't you see, Josie? This is just like before."

"No, Michael, I don't see that at all." This time Josie stepped back, being careful not to trip over the skirt of Gran's gown. Only a few feet separated them, but it felt like a thousand miles.

"You lose your job and then you tell me you're going to stay in Tulsa and marry me. You took the easy way out. After all these years, you still don't know what you really want."

Josie placed her hands on her hips, feeling her blood pressure rise with her anger. "That's not true. I know exactly what I want. I made that decision before Anne Devon arrived." When he wouldn't look her in the eye, she knew he doubted her, and she couldn't live with a man who didn't trust her.

Shaking her finger at him, she said, "I'll take the blame for walking out seven years ago. That was my fault. But this time, it's your fault Michael. You're the one making the big mistake."

"I'm sorry," he said. "Please, give me my ring back."

Josie tugged on the emerald ring, but her fingers were so clammy it wouldn't budge past her first knuckle. She stopped trying for a moment and said, "I don't know why you want it back now. Just because we've broken up doesn't mean I'll abandon Sharla. We're still pretending we're engaged."

Michael shook his head, and when she met his gaze she realized how deeply troubled he was.

"You're right," he said. "I did make the mistake. I didn't trust God to make the right decision for Sharla. I was so afraid of losing her that I took matters into my own hands. I should never have asked you to go along with a fake engagement. How can God honor my devious ways?"

Josie had no answer. That was a question she, too, struggled with.

"From now on, I want to proceed with honesty and integrity. And if I'm awarded custody of Sharla, I'll know I truly deserved the court's confidence."

Josie pulled on the ring until her finger turned red, and she didn't give up until it slipped from her finger.

When she placed the emerald ring in Michael's hand, their fingers touched briefly. As she ran from the room, she caught her reflection in the cheval glass. What they said really was true. It was very unlucky for the groom to see the bride in her wedding dress before the wedding ceremony.

After two sleepless nights, Josie was awakened before sunrise by the telephone, then a light knock on her door. "It's for you," her mother said. "A Ms. Myers."

"Marsha Myers?" Josie asked, sitting up quickly.

"She didn't say."

Josie picked up the extension in her room. To her surprise her mother remained in the doorway. It wasn't like Sarah to invade her privacy.

"News certainly travels fast," Josie said, as she listened to Marsha's excited voice.

"Yes...really? Are you certain? Can I think about it?" Josie asked.

She met her mother's gaze as she said, "I'll let you know by the end of the day."

As soon as she hung up the telephone, Sarah said, "Well?"

"Marsha Myers is the director of a charity very similar to the one I've been working for that is headquartered in Switzerland. When they heard I was unemployed, they wanted me to know I had a place with them."

"And are you really considering their offer?" Sarah crossed her arms over her chest emphasizing her disapproval.

"I told them I would think about it. I know you don't want me to leave."

"What I don't want is for you to make the biggest mistake of your life."

"Mom, it's just not going to work between me and Michael. We tried. But it's just not meant to be." Josie spoke firmly, though she didn't believe her speech any more than her mother did. She and Michael were meant to be together. "But just because I'm not going to marry him, doesn't mean I'm going to leave Tulsa." Though living in the same town with him wouldn't be easy. But if she was going to live the life God had planned for her, she had to quit running from Michael.

Sarah dropped her arms to her side. "Well, now you're talking sense."

"I'm ready to come home," she said. "And even if my relationship with Michael is over, I want to be here with you and Dad and Gran. I'm ready to put down roots in a community. I'm glad I worked with the charity, and like you've always said, there are plenty of children right here in Tulsa who need me."

"But?" her mother asked.

"But, I do have to consider the request. It's a great opportunity."

Sarah took her daughter's hands in hers, and said, "You and Michael belong together. Don't run. Fight for him."

Josie sighed, wishing it were as simple as her mother seemed to think.

With hands on her hips, Sarah said, "I have no doubt God called you home this summer in order to bring you and Michael back together. Neither of you would have gone along with this fake engagement if you didn't still love each other."

"What are you talking about?" Josie asked.

"Come on, we all know you're trying to help Michael gain custody of Sharla."

"But how did you know?"

Sarah squeezed her daughter's hands tightly. "Because we know you and Michael. And we know that you truly do love each other in the way a husband and wife love."

"Oh, Mom," Josie said. "Are you mad at us for deceiving you?"

Sarah's eyes sparkled with delight. "Are you kidding? I saw this as a great opportunity to make sure you and Michael really did get married."

Josie shook her head. "That's not going to happen."

"It's not over," Sarah promised.

Should she stay or go?

Josie sipped a hot cup of coffee as she swung on the backyard swing. The beautiful coo of an unseen mourning dove comforted her soul as she sought God in prayer.

Just two days ago, she'd been so certain she should stay. But Michael's rejection had caused her to reexamine her motives, and now she found herself back where she'd started.

But that wasn't true, either. She wasn't the same woman who'd come home almost six weeks ago. Her trust in God now anchored her daily life in a way she'd never experienced before.

As she continued to swing and pray, the decision

finally became clear. God hadn't called her home to Tulsa to seek a new direction for her life. He'd called her home because Tulsa was where she belonged.

And Michael was wrong. They weren't replaying history, and she knew how to prove it to him. Seven years ago, they'd both given up without a fight, but not this time. Sarah's words echoed in her mind: *It's not over yet.*

Leaving the empty coffee mug on the swing, Josie ran toward Michael's house. When she knocked on the front door, no one answered. She knocked again. Silence. She ran to the back door and knocked. Again silence. She twisted the doorknob and discovered it was unlocked. "Michael," she called out.

Glancing at the kitchen clock, she realized it was nearly time for the custody hearing. He must have left early, she thought. She ran to the front of the house just to make certain he wasn't there. "Michael," she yelled again.

When she turned toward the living room, she gasped. Envelopes and paper were strewn across the hardwood floor. Curious, she knelt down to gather the letters. Recognizing her own handwriting, she froze. As her eyes drifted from letter to letter, she knew she would never again doubt his love.

She started to pick up the letters and then decided she didn't have time if she was going to get to the courthouse before the custody hearing began. She dropped the letters onto the open rolltop desk, and when she did, she saw the emerald ring. Without hesitation, she slipped the ring on her finger.

Dear Lord, she prayed, *don't let it be too late.*

Josie ran across the long parking lot to the main courthouse entrance. Just inside the heavy double doors, she paused long enough to read the wall directory. "Room 505," she chanted to herself as she raced there.

Outside room 505, she paused long enough to take a deep breath and pray she'd arrived before Michael told the caseworker they were no longer engaged. Twisting the emerald engagement ring with her thumb, she pushed open the doors to family court.

Though the room was small, it looked as she'd expected with a judge's bench, tables for the plaintiffs and defendants, as well as an empty jury box and a small public seating area. Josie quickly took roll. Eddie, his wife and his attorney huddled in a back corner, while Michael and his attorney were already seated. The judge, as well as the court officers, had yet to arrive. Josie sighed loudly. Anne Devon was nowhere in sight.

Hearing the doors behind her open, Josie turned and looked directly at Anne. She flashed the woman a quick smile, and then hurried up the aisle to Michael. Just as she tapped him on the shoulder, the judge entered the courtroom.

"We've got to talk," she whispered to Michael, hoping to avoid a scene in the quiet room.

"Not now," he said. "Please, leave." Worry darkened his eyes and tightened his brow. Judging by the dark circles under his eyes, he hadn't slept peacefully since he'd demanded she give back his grandmother's engagement ring.

"I'm staying, Michael," she said.

"Josie...this isn't the time—"

"I'm staying in Tulsa. I've never been more certain of what I want in my entire life. I want to spend the rest of my life with you," she whispered.

Hope grew in Michael's eyes as he began to understand what she was saying.

"I love you with all my heart," she said. "We belong together, Michael—you, me and Sharla." Josie swallowed hard as hot blood raced through her veins. The small room closed in around Michael and herself as everyone else faded from her vision.

"Do you mean...are you saying..."

"Michael, will you marry me?" she whispered loud enough for only his ears.

"Yes," he shouted, grabbing her by the waist and hugging her until she felt as though they'd become one.

The judge cleared his throat. "If you two could save the cuddling for later, I would like to get started."

Josie sat behind Michael in the empty public seating area. The custody hearing passed quickly as she clutched the emerald ring and prayed for the judge to exercise divine wisdom. For as she listened to the attorneys present their cases, she realized that only God could see into the future and know what was best for Sharla.

After what seemed like forever, the judge announced his decision. Josie leaned forward and placed her hand on Michael's shoulder. Instantly, he covered her hand with his and squeezed until she thought she would faint.

"This has not been an easy decision as both the child's biological father and Michael Rawlins have much to offer her. However, I feel it is in the child's best interest to grant full custody to Michael Rawlins, with liberal visitation to Eddie Lewis."

The judge continued, but Josie didn't hear another word. At the sound of the gavel, she jumped up and threw her arms around Michael.

With tears streaming down his face, Michael said, "It's official, we're going to be parents. Are you sure you're up for the challenge?" Michael asked, his voice rich with emotion.

Josie nodded. "Being an instant mother will be a challenge, but with God's blessing and your love, I know I can do it."

Michael pushed a strand of hair from her face, then caressed her cheek with the back of his hand. "I don't have a single doubt. You'll be a wonderful mother."

Just as he kissed her lightly on the lips, her parents and Gran entered the courtroom.

"We couldn't stay away," Mrs. Marshall declared.

"It's good news," Josie said. "We're a family. The judge granted Michael full custody."

"The judge granted *us* full custody," Michael corrected. Then with amusement in his eyes added, "I think the judge knew the second he walked in and saw you in my arms that we had more than enough love for Sharla...as well as all the brothers and sisters we're going to give her!"

Overwhelmed with joy, Josie looked upward and uttered a silent prayer. *Thank You, Lord, for bringing me home to the man I love.*

Chapter Fifteen

"**A**re you ready?" Josie's father asked as he held out his arm for his daughter.

"I've been ready since the day I met Michael." She smiled with a confidence that filled her heart.

"Then we've got a wedding to go to."

As her father led her down her parents' back steps, the "Wedding March" filled the air. When they reached the ground, Mr. Marshall paused for a moment and looked at Josie with such pride and love that she felt her knees buckle. Placing one hand on the nearby railing, she steadied herself.

"I've never seen you look more beautiful," he said.

"Thank you, Daddy."

"And you don't know how happy you've made your mother by wearing her wedding suit."

"As happy as it makes me to wear this suit," she assured him.

Josie tugged on the fitted jacket, and then raising the bouquet of white roses and baby's breath to her nose, she inhaled the wondrous fragrance.

It'd been Gran's suggestion that she try on her mother's suit, and the idea had instantly appealed to Josie...

"After all, Michael's seen you in my wedding gown."

"And no offense, Gran, but that wasn't one of my better days."

At first, her mother had been reluctant, but when Josie had convinced her she was serious, they'd removed the white suit from storage.

"It's incredible, Mother," Josie'd exclaimed. As soon as she slipped into the straight skirt and short jacket, she knew this was the perfect wedding outfit. With its fitted waist, narrow peplum and seed pearls covering the cuffs and lapel, she felt more elegant and beautiful than she'd ever dreamed possible.

Sarah asked once again, "Are you certain you don't want a large church wedding? I've always thought you would wear Gran's dress."

Taking her mother's hands, Josie said, "I'm positive. I want to be married in Michael's backyard. And it only seems right that we should pledge our love to each other before God on the steps of Sharla's playhouse. If it hadn't been for her,

*Michael and I might never have found our way back
to each other.''*

''If you're sure, then,'' Sarah said.

''You and Daddy got off to a great start with a
simple wedding, and so will Michael and I.'' Josie
hugged her mother, praying that just as she'd grown
into her mother's suit that she would also continue
to grow into the maturity of her mother's faith...

A quick squeeze of her father's hand brought
Josie back to the present.

''Thanks, too, for letting your mother plan this
wedding.''

''We could never have gone ahead on such short
notice without yours and Mother's help.''

''You know we're always here for you.''

Biting down on her bottom lip Josie nodded,
afraid to speak for fear she would burst into tears.

Together they walked across the driveway and
through the shrub archway that had been decorated
with white roses.

Their family and closest friends stood as Josie and
her father walked down the white carpet to the playhouse steps. Waiting ahead were one of Michael's
brothers-in-law and her dear friend, Stephanie, who
together served as best man and matron of honor,
and Sharla, who carried a basket of daisies, as she
held Michael's hand.

When Josie's gaze met Michael's she could no
longer hold back the tears. They were so fortunate
God had given them a second chance.

"Dearly beloved," Reverend Conner began. "We have gathered here today for this most joyous occasion..."

Standing next to Michael, with Sharla a half a step ahead of them both, Josie marveled at how she'd had to travel halfway around the world in order to realize the love of her life lived next door.

"...I now pronounce you man and wife...and a family," Reverend Conner proclaimed.

A year later

"Mamma, can we watch the wedding video?" Sharla stood next to the television holding the videotape.

"Again?" Josie asked.

Sharla nodded enthusiastically.

"If you insist."

In the last year, Sharla had watched the wedding tape so many times Josie had made several copies for fear the child would wear out the original tape.

However, it thrilled her that Sharla loved the tape, and like her daughter, Josie never tired of replaying her wedding day.

Josie pushed the tape into the recorder and pushed the Play button. The camera focused on Michael's backyard, slowly panning on family and friends who sat on white wooden chairs as the "Wedding March" played, then zooming in on the Victorian playhouse with its stained-glass windows and gingerbread trim.

On the couch, Sharla snuggled close to Josie as they both relived the day.

While Josie walked down the aisle on tape, Sharla said, "Do you remember the first time you met me?"

"Of course," Josie said. "It was one of the most important days of my life." When her daughter was older, Josie planned to tell Sharla the important role she'd played in helping Josie and Michael rediscover their love.

"Do you know what I prayed for that day?"

Josie shook her head, remembering the morning Michael had taken her to Grandmother Rubee's house. While she'd loved Sharla instantly, there'd been no way she could have known how quickly and deeply her love for the child would grow once she'd adopted Sharla.

"I prayed you would be my mother. I figured since God took my first mother home to heaven that He ought to let me pick my second mother."

With damp eyes, Josie marveled at the young child's faith and knew this girl would teach her as much about life as Angelina had.

"Well, I'm glad you picked me," Josie said, pulling Sharla close. "I love you."

She thought of the letter Michael had given her after the judge had made his ruling. Knowing she had Denise's blessing meant the world to her.

"I love you, too," Sharla whispered. Then raising her head, she said, "I think I hear Dad's car."

A few minutes later, the back door slammed shut, followed by footsteps down the hallway. "Honey, I'm home," Michael called out.

"We're in the living room."

"Wow, what smells so good?" Michael said as he came around the corner.

"Mamma and I made your favorite—chocolate chip cookies," Sharla said, beaming with pride.

As Josie embraced her husband, she suddenly remembered the day, just a little over a year ago, when she'd used the hidden key to let herself into Michael's house and had imagined being married to him. On that day, a future with Michael had seemed impossible.

So much had changed in the last year. Not only had she become a wife and a mother, but with the support of her local church, she'd started an organization that provided relief for single-parent families.

But one thing had never changed—the love she and Michael shared. And with God's blessing, their love would last a lifetime.

* * * * *

Dear Reader,

I hope you enjoyed Josie and Michael's story as much as I enjoyed writing it. This will always be a very special book for me as I wrote it during my mother's fight against cancer. I named Josie after my mother because I owe my writing career to her. From the time I learned to read until I was old enough to drive, Mom and I made bimonthly visits to the Tompkins County Library, which was a half hour from our home in upstate New York. Though we'd always shared a passion for books, it wasn't until years later when I'd started writing that Mom told me being a writer had always been her secret dream. Though she didn't live long enough to see her dream fulfilled, she was able to help me celebrate the sale of *With All Josie's Heart* to Steeple Hill.

Thanks again for letting me share my story with you. If you'd like to write me, you can reach me at 5147 South Harvard, PMB 119, Tulsa, Oklahoma, 74135.

All my best,

Next month from Steeple Hill's

Love Inspired®

LOVE SIGN
by

Susan Kirby

Author Shelby Taylor drives off to the country in search of peace and quiet after her fiancé jilts her. But at a rest stop, her car is smashed by a sign truck. When handsome Jake Jackson offers Shelby his family's hospitality until her car can be fixed, sparks fly between them. Will Shelby stop writing her book long enough to see what God has in store for her?

**Don't miss
LOVE SIGN
On sale February 2001**

Love Inspired®

LILS

Next month
from Steeple Hill's

Love Inspired

AUTUMN'S AWAKENING
by

Irene Brand

Veterinarian Autumn Weaver returns home to her
family farm and runs into old love Nathan Holland.
He remembers the spoiled teenager she once was, and
is wary to trust her now. When they must join forces
to save a horse's life, Nathan soon realizes Autumn
has grown into a beautiful, mature woman.
Can they find true happiness together?

Don't miss
AUTUMN'S AWAKENING
On sale February 2001

Visit us at www.steeplehill.com

LIAA